SON OF
THE MOB

SON OF THE MOB

GORDON KORMAN

HYPERION
Los Angeles   New York

Copyright © 2002 by Gordon Korman

All rights reserved. Published by Hyperion, an imprint of Disney Book Group. No part of this book may be reproduced or transmitted in any form or by any means, electronic or mechanical, including photocopying, recording, or by any information storage and retrieval system, without written permission from the publisher. For information address Hyperion, 125 West End Avenue, New York, New York 10023.

First Hardcover Edition, October 2002
First Paperback Edition, September 2004
New Paperback Edition, June 2017

10 9 8 7 6 5 4 3 2 1
FAC-025438-17132
Printed in the United States of America

This book is set in 11.5-point Janson Text LT Pro/Fontspring

Library of Congress Control Number for Hardcover Edition: 2002068672
ISBN 978-1-4847-9845-4
Visit www.hyperionteens.com

SUSTAINABLE
FORESTRY
INITIATIVE
Certified Chain of Custody
Promoting Sustainable Forestry
www.sfiprogram.org
SFI-01054
The SFI label applies to the text stock

For Alessandra Balzer,
my partner in crime

SON OF THE MOB

[ONE]

THE WORST NIGHT OF MY LIFE? My first—and last—date with Angela O'Bannon.

Here's how it goes down:

Five o'clock. I'm already nervous by the time Alex drops by to go over the checklist. Alex is always pretty skittish around my family because of what my father does for a living. Especially since my older brother Tommy, who works for Dad, is hanging around. Tommy's on the warpath, storming through the house like a caged tiger, and ranting about how Benny the Zit is supposed to be here to pick him up for some business or other. Real pleasant.

Once I shut the door to my room, though, Alex is all calm efficiency.

"Car keys?" he barks.

"Check."

"Money?"

"Check."

"Blanket?"

That's for Bryce Beach, where, if all goes well, and with a little help from above, I'll be able to maneuver Angela at the end of the night.

"It's in the trunk," I assure him. "Everything's going to be fine."

"Don't get cocky!" he snaps at me. "This is my love life we're talking about!"

That's Alex's new thing. Since he has no love life, he wants to score vicariously through me. Except I have no love life either. Until tonight, maybe.

Alex's probing eyes fall on the neatly folded sweater on my bed. Every article of clothing in my closet has the same preppy look—my mom's idea of what I should appear to be. Appearances are big with her. Understandable, under the circumstances.

"Vince, you're not wearing *that*?" he says.

"Yeah. Why?"

He slaps his forehead. "It's *wool*! Scratchy! You're taking her to a horror movie! She's going to be all over you! We need one-hundred-percent cotton, or maybe a nice linen-silk blend. . . ."

By the time we pick out an appropriate outfit and go over the last few rules of engagement ("Don't order the chili! All our hard work falls apart if your stomach's gurgling with swamp gas!"), it's almost six. Alex takes off, and I run down to the basement for a quick workout on the Universal gym. Don't get me wrong. I'm no musclehead. But I kind of enjoy the exercise when I've got something on my mind. Your brain shifts down, narrowing its function to the tiny task of lifting the weight from *here* to *there*. It's like therapy. And it wouldn't hurt to grow myself a pair of shoulders, for God's sake. The Lucas are built like trucks. How did I come out a beanpole, especially when Mom cooks from the *How to Feed an Army and Still Have Leftovers* recipe book? Once, I tried to get her to admit I was adopted. After all, wasn't I the only Luca male with no interest in the family business? But she assured me I was legit—which is more than she could say for the family business. Not that she ever admits to that.

Anyway, I shower up and hit the road. Even from the driveway I can hear my windbag brother inside in the den tearing a strip off Benny the Zit, who finally showed up, I guess. What I don't know at that point is that while I was working out, Tommy got sick of waiting for Benny, borrowed my car, and went to attend to that business on his own. That's why he's yelling—because Benny stood him up.

With Alex's advice and my brother's tantrum ringing in my ears, I go to pick up Angela. She looks *awesome*—even better than at school, with a little extra makeup, and a low-cut sweater and skintight pants instead of the baggy shirts and jeans that have almost turned into a uniform at Jefferson High. We go to eat at the Coffee Shop, which is actually a really cool restaurant designed to look like an old-fashioned diner. I order the chili. Yeah, I know Alex warned against it, but things are going great, and my confidence is growing by the minute—another Luca family trait; maybe I wasn't adopted after all. I mean, the food's good, Angela seems to be into me, and the conversation is really flowing. Alex spent the last day and a half surfing Internet chat rooms and prepping me with dozens of topics I could bring up if the table ever got uncomfortably quiet.

"This is my love life here," Alex reminded me. "I can't risk you getting dissed because she thinks you've got nothing to talk about."

"Maybe if you didn't spend all your time on the Internet, you'd have your *own* love life," I shot back at him.

I feel kind of bad about that later at the movie, with Angela locked on to me like a boa constrictor in spandex. I won't admit it to Alex, but I barely even notice she's there. What kind of a sick, demented screenwriter could have ever dreamed up a story like *Harvest of Death*? There are seventeen main characters, and by the time thirty minutes have passed, they're all dead, including the killer. He, as near as I can tell, is a cross between a vampire and a hay-baling machine. Just when I'm thinking there's no one left to be in the rest of the movie, along comes a troop of Girl Guides menaced by the vampire's evil twin—yes, the first killer was the *good* guy, or the good hay baler. Take your pick.

Well, the movie must have done the trick, because when I suggest we hit the beach, Angela's back in the car before I can finish stammering out "B-bryce B-beach." So much for the extensive begging, cajoling, and negotiating Alex prepared me for.

I'm a little worried by all the other traffic going our way. Bryce Beach is a popular spot for the high schools in our area. Will we be able to find any privacy?

"Park over there," Angela says decisively, pointing to a spot shielded by two outcroppings of the dunes.

I can't help suspecting she's been here before. She's a woman with *experience*. We get out of the car and stand silhouetted in the moonlight as the surf pounds against the shore, and a whispering wind . . . you get the picture. I'll never describe it right. I'm a Luca. Anything more than a series of grunts is considered eloquence from us. The point is, everything's perfect, as if the Supreme Power has stepped in to set it all up for me.

She kisses me—the kind of kiss you feel in the tips of your toes. The kind of kiss that conveys the promise of everything that comes along with it.

"Got a blanket or something?"

"Everything is provided for your comfort," I manage to croak. I'm not proud of the feeble attempt to be suave. But after that kiss, I'm amazed my mouth works at all.

I pop the trunk, reach in, and freeze. I almost choke on my lungs, which have leaped up the back of my throat. There's the blanket, all right—wrapped around the unconscious body of some guy! To be honest, my first thought is that he's dead—which isn't such a stretch; I told you about the family business. But when I suck in air with a resounding wheeze that echoes down the beach, his thin-lipped mouth lets out a little moan.

"I'm *wait-ing*," Angela teases in a playful singsong voice. She has her arms wrapped lightly around herself, chilled by the sea breeze.

"Be right there," I rasp. I *know* this person. James Ratelli—Jimmy Rat. He owns a sleazy nightclub on the Lower East Side. Borrowed money from my father to get it started up.

My father. They call him Honest Abe Luca instead of

Anthony because he's so straight in his business dealings, no matter how illegal they may happen to be. Never rips anybody off. Never breaks a promise. Except one: Honest Abe just can't seem to make good on his word to keep his line of work completely separate from my life. And now I'm stranded on Bryce Beach with a red-hot and revved-up Angela O'Bannon in my arms and an out-cold Jimmy Rat in the trunk of my Mazda Protegé.

It looks like my brother worked him over pretty good, too. Tommy's going to pay to dry-clean that blanket, but there's no time to think about that here.

Now, this doesn't exactly put me in the mood for love, but I've got to stall for time, and I can only think of one way to do it. I clamp myself onto Angela like there's no tomorrow. I guess she misinterprets my desperation as grand passion and starts kissing me—I mean, really going nuts at it. *There's* a strategy I'll bet Alex never considered for his checklist.

So here I am, getting the best action of my life. But I can't even enjoy it, because six feet away, the trunk is open and Jimmy Rat is snoring softly and bleeding all over my blanket.

At this point, I'm committed to a course of action. I try to ease Angela down to the beach, but she pulls away. "Get the blanket!"

"The beach is nice and soft—"

"I don't want sand all over me!" she exclaims, furthering my suspicion that she's an old hand at this. She dances around me, and before I can stop her, she's staring into the trunk at the blanket and its current occupant.

Well, don't even ask about the screaming. I thought

Harvest of Death was bad, but this is in a whole other league. I guess being mauled by a vampire-hay baler is nothing compared to finding a body in your make-out blanket.

"He's dead! He's dead! Oh my God, Vince, he's dead!"

"He's not dead." For some reason, the only thing I can think of is that old dead parrot skit on Monty Python. "He's—resting."

Angela spares me the tough questions. She just gets in the car, arms folded, face like stone. "Take me home, Vince. This minute."

What can I do? I slam down the trunk lid, climb behind the wheel, and put the car in gear.

"I'm really sorry about this, Angela."

Her silence is even more deafening than the screaming a couple minutes before.

That's when I see the traffic jam. Oh, no! The cops have set up a roadblock on the causeway. They're searching cars coming off the beach, looking for booze and drugs. I haven't got any of that stuff. What I *do* have is Jimmy Rat, in used condition.

I throw the Mazda into reverse, but by that time, there are a couple of cars in line behind me. Besides, this is the route off the beach, period. The only other escape is by submarine.

I have a giddy vision of Alex, continuing his checklist: *Snorkel mask?*

Snorkel mask? What for?

For when you get caught with a body in the trunk, and you have to swim for it. Don't get cocky, Vince. This is my love life we're talking about!

The guy three cars ahead of me gets nailed with a bottle of vodka, but he passes the Breathalyzer. They chew him out and confiscate the booze, but he doesn't get arrested.

No such hope for me. They're not likely to confiscate Jimmy Rat and send me off with a warning. Especially not after they see the name *Luca* on my driver's license. My family has quite a reputation in law-enforcement circles.

"Let me do all the talking," I whisper to Angela. Like there's anything to say.

She nods, petrified. At least our predicament has scared her into forgetting how mad she is.

The roadblock is two cars away. Now one. Beside me, Angela's lips are moving. I think she's praying.

The Nissan in front pulls away. It's our turn.

And then—an act of God.

Horn honking wildly, an out-of-control Cadillac weaves down the causeway from the other direction, doing at least sixty. All at once, the driver slams on the brakes. The wheels lock, sending the big car into a spin. It sideswipes the divider in a metal-on-metal shower of sparks, and lurches to a halt. There, hanging onto the wheel for dear life, sits Benny the Zit. He's looking straight at me through the crack in his windshield.

The cops all leap the divider and run to the scene of the accident.

Hey, I'm not going to wait for an engraved invitation. I stomp on the accelerator and get out of there. About fifteen other cars peel off after me.

I get the real story later. When my dad found out that I'd

gone on a date with Jimmy Rat in the trunk of my Mazda, he gave my brother a major earache. Well, Tommy passed the pain on to Benny. After all, it was Benny's fault that Tommy had to take my car to lean on Jimmy Rat. So it became Benny's job to get me out of this, no matter what the cost. The cost turned out to be one Cadillac.

In my family, this counts as justice.

Our thrilling escape does nothing to thaw Angela's icy attitude toward me. When I drop her off at her house, she says, "If you promise not to call me; not to talk to me; to pass me in the hall and not even *look* in my direction; then maybe—*maybe*—I'll forget what was in your trunk tonight."

I nod sadly. "I've never seen you before in my life." And I drive away.

From the trunk of the Mazda, I hear pounding. Jimmy Rat wants out. I know I'm going to catch hell for this from Tommy, but I pull over and free the guy. I notice for the first time that he isn't wearing any pants, so I let him keep the blanket. I even give him change for the phone so he can call a cab.

He looks disdainfully at my Mazda. "Damn foreign cars. No trunk space at all."

I have to keep myself from telling him, *Hey, blame Benny the Zit. If he hadn't been late, you could have been beaten up and imprisoned in the back of a Cadillac—the Ritz-Carlton of trunks. Would that have been suitable?*

So that's the whole story, the postmortem, pardon the expression. It's the right one, though. A postmortem is done on a dead body. And nothing is deader than the relationship between Angela O'Bannon and me.

According to Alex the next day, all this is my fault.

"Face it, Vince. You screwed up. You had a golden opportunity, and you blew it. This isn't doing my love life any good, you know."

Think what it's doing to mine.

[TWO]

I **WAS ABOUT FOUR WHEN** I first started to realize that my family wasn't like the families of some of my friends at preschool.

Mom is bundling me out of the house to catch the bus when I turn and ask, "Where's Daddy?"

"He's sleeping, Vincent. You'll see him when you come home for lunch."

I point up and down the street. "But all the other daddies go to work. They drive in their cars, or they take the train to the city."

Here's what she tells me: "Your father's in the vending-machine business. He works different hours because you never know when a vending machine is going to break."

That's her explanation for why Dad has to run off at two o'clock in the morning on urgent business. I honestly used to believe that somewhere there was a jammed-up soda machine, and my dad had to rush off in the dead of night and fix it. Hey, I was four.

Brothers Vending Machines, Inc. is the name of the

company. I always thought that was pretty strange considering Dad's an only child. But even though he has no brothers, there were always lots of uncles around. I made a list once. I was up to sixty before I gave up. And some of the names! I have an Uncle Fingers, Uncle Puke, Uncle Shank, Uncle Fin, Uncle Pampers, and Uncle Exit. I have two uncles named Nose—Big-Nose and No-Nose. I even have an Uncle named Uncle. Everybody calls him that, except his real nephews, who call him T-Bird.

Seven years old: I wake up for a drink of water and find blood-spattered towels in the bathtub. Scared out of my mind, I run to my parents' room to find the light on and a little meatball surgery in progress. There's plastic sheeting over everything. My uncle Carmine lies facedown on the bed, crying and whimpering. My dad sits on him to hold him still, while my mother digs at him with a tweezers.

"Aha!" she exclaims, coming up with a tiny misshapen object covered in gore.

Uncle Carmine screams bloody murder.

"Shut up, Carmine!" orders my father. "If you wake the kids, the next one's going in your head."

They tell me it's a kidney stone, but I'm not fooled.

My teacher, Mrs. Metzger, confirms my suspicion that kidney stones don't come out of your butt cheek.

The peculiarities begin to mount up. The sudden "school camping trip" where none of the other kids are from my class. And where one day, I open my Cracker Jacks at snack time and find a box full of cut diamonds. Everybody else has a ball while I sit in the cabin, guarding my cache of "snacks," afraid to open anything else. I have to be evaluated by a psychologist after that, because I'm so obsessed with my food.

When I get back to my own school, none of the kids in my class have gone on any camping trip. They think I've been out with strep throat.

Dad says special cleaners were working in our house while I was away, so he had to get rid of the Cracker Jacks because it's so messy. Those guys must have been pretty lousy cleaners, because they cut open every teddy bear in my closet.

Stuff like that.

By this point, Tommy has already told me, "Dad's mobbed up." But back then I assumed it just meant he had a lot of friends.

He's such a fun father. While all the uncles ignore their kids, Dad always finds time for Tommy and me, and our older sister, Mira. He teases us, and cracks great jokes, and we always get tons of presents. There are these fun little rituals, too. Every night before he shuts out the lights in the den, he'll look up and address the fixture: "And a special good night to you, Agent Numb-Nuts." Or he'll call into the garage, "We're going out to dinner if it's all right with you, Agent Needledink. Should I bring you a doggie bag?"

As a kid, I thought it was a riot. It's only now, years later, that I realize Dad's talking to real people. FBI agents, to be specific. Our house was—and still is—always bugged.

I'll never forget the day it sank in that people are out there listening. Every burp, every trip to the can, and worse—all preserved on tape by federal agents. Home sweet home.

At least now I understand why Dad flips his lid the day

I accidentally open up that suitcase full of bearer bonds.

"What's this, Dad? It looks like some kind of money."

The father who never so much as smacked my behind clamps a death grip on my mouth with the strength of the jaws of a great white shark.

"It's play money, Vince. Like Monopoly."

Uncle Cosimo, who's in charge of the suitcase, cuts our lawn for the next three summers.

Think what a terrible burden it is for a high-school kid: if you say the wrong thing in the privacy of your own home, you might end up sending your father to prison.

One day I corner Mom in the laundry room, where the roar of the washer covers our conversation. "I know what Dad does for a living."

She nods. "He's an excellent provider. Thank God, vending machines are a profitable business."

"Oh, Mom," I complain. "Don't treat me like an idiot. I know he's in the Mob."

She stares at me, shocked. "What on earth are you talking about?"

"Come on, Mom. I know you know!"

I've got to give her credit. She never retreats an inch. Either that or my poor mother is so dumb that, ten years ago, she really did believe that Uncle Carmine passed a kidney stone through a bloody hole in his left buttock. It's a mean thing to say about your mom, but I have to consider heredity. There must be an explanation for Tommy, after all. And Mira majored in media studies, not astrophysics, in community college.

My mother can serve a sit-down dinner for fifteen guys at four in the morning with ten minutes' advance notice. Our basement is full of freezers packed with food just in case the Mormon Tabernacle Choir drops by in the state she prefers all her guests to be in—ravenous. And her cooking is great, if a little heavy. Not just in your stomach. Try *carrying* it. A Tupperware container of Mom's lasagna weighs twice as much as anybody else's.

That's not to say that Mom and her meatballs are all meat and no balls. I remember once there was this guy, Angelo, a real young Turk in Uncle Shank's crew, who had some kind of beef with Tommy. This is right after Tommy quit school to join the business, so he was about my age now, and nowhere near as tough as his current, put-Jimmy-Rat-in-the-trunk self.

Dad absolutely refuses to intervene on his son's behalf. "If I mix in, you'll never command any respect on your own," he says. But Tommy keeps getting pushed around. A few weeks later, Uncle Shank and his guys are over at the house, and Mom asks Angelo to "help her" in the kitchen. They're alone in there together, and suddenly there's the most God-awful scream coming from Angelo. He leaves in a hurry, and we order Chinese food that night—an event so rare that it should come with skywriting and fireworks.

"I thought we were having chicken potpie," I say.

"The potpie," she tells me, "is totally out of commission."

I don't push it. *Totally out of commission* is a phrase Mom uses to describe things that are gone, finished, and never to be seen again on this earth. Although, in this case, I do see the potpie again. There it is, in the garbage, dish and all. The crust is broken in a perfect handprint. Coincidentally, Angelo walks around with a bandaged hand for six weeks. First-degree burns.

The incident is never mentioned at our house, but from that day on I realize that Mom has a titanium backbone to go with her heart of gold. And if food is her medium, it can also be her message. Where family is concerned, nobody messes with Mom, not even her powerful husband.

Angelo never bugged Tommy again. A few months later, he stopped hanging around Uncle Shank and his crew. They say he moved out west.

Alex, who is turned to stone in the presence of Dad, Tommy, or any of the uncles, always has plenty to say when we're alone. "Don't you ever watch Mafia movies? Do you have any idea the kind of *chicks* these guys get? I defy you to show me one gangster with an ugly girlfriend."

To say Alex has a one-track mind is an insult to one-track minds.

"You're practically a Mob prince," he presses on. "There must be some way to use that to rustle us up a couple of dates!"

"That is *never* going to be a part of my life!" I vow. "I've had it out with my dad, and he knows exactly how I feel."

He looks at me in awe. "Really? What did he say?"

It was less than a year ago. Dad doesn't say anything at first, and it isn't just because of our latest FBI eavesdropper, Agent Bite-Me. We're in my father's basement workshop, the one room in our house that's guaranteed safe. With unfinished concrete walls and floor, there's virtually nowhere to hide a listening device. It's Tommy's job as Dad's apprentice to sweep the tools and equipment for bugs twice a day. That includes the Universal gym, and the woodworking area. A lot of conferences take place there, and a lot of uncles make their way down the basement stairs.

He sits me in a rickety, lopsided wooden chair that rocks precariously on the concrete floor. Why do the well-to-do Lucas have such a piece of junk in their upscale home? Because it's an Anthony Luca handmade special. For years, Dad has been talking about not working so hard, scaling back his day-to-day involvement in the business, stopping to smell the roses, blah, blah, blah. Uncle Sal recently died (actually, I think he had help) and it reminded Dad that life is short.

So my father took up woodworking to relax him. He threw himself into his new hobby with the intense determination that characterizes everything else he does. And he has to be maybe the lousiest carpenter on the planet.

But he doesn't know that. He's Anthony Luca. Who's going to tell him? I've seen some of the toughest wiseguys in the tristate area oohing and aahing over a napkin holder that would languish on the shelf of the 99-cent shop.

"So," he begins, "you're not interested in the vending-machine business."

I start to argue, but decide, What's the point? We both know what we're talking about. "Yeah, vending machines," I say. "It's a little tough for my tastes."

Dad breathes a heavy sigh. He knows I don't approve of

his line of work, but I think he always hoped I'd grow out of it. As if obeying the law is a silly phase some crazy kids experiment with, like smoking cigars or racing motorcycles. "A man has the right to choose his own destiny," he acknowledges. "So now we know what you don't want. Tell me what you do want."

My mind goes blank. He smiles, as if he's expecting that. "When I was your age, Vince, we had nothing. So I was the most motivated guy in the world to get out there and do better than my old man. With you it's different. You've got a great deal here—nice house, room service, new car. . . ." I drove a Porsche back then (sixteenth birthday present) until the cops came and took it away to give back to the guy who really owned it.

"I've got ambition," I interrupt. "I just haven't figured out what I'm ambitious about yet."

"The law's a nice career for a kid with the gift of gab," he suggests. "You can never have too many lawyers."

"You've got Mel," I remind him. Mira's husband. He just started working for Dad.

My father shrugs. "Mel's my son-in-law. You're blood."

"You don't get it," I insist. "I don't want to be involved, period. I don't want 'vending machines' touching my life in any way."

He looks amused. "Too late. You think we'd live the way we do if I was in any other business? You're already in it, Vince. Right down to the clothes you wear, the food you eat, your allowance . . ." He pauses. "What you say makes sense. If you're not motivated by what I do, then fine. But you're seventeen years old now. It's time to get motivated about *something*."

That's classic Dad—reasonable, sensible, supportive. People who meet him outside of business find it hard to believe that this classy, soft-spoken gentleman is who he is. It only becomes clear when you see how the uncles tiptoe around him, the fear in people's faces when they hear his name, the scrambling that goes on when he asks for something. It's only at those times that I realize the great guy I call Dad is a man who runs a criminal organization that operates by means of violence and intimidation. And I really, truly, honestly want nothing to do with it.

The funny thing is that, for a Mob boss, my dad is considered the most ethical and trustworthy man alive. He really is Honest Abe Luca—although I don't know if our sixteenth president would have appreciated the comparison.

Tommy says the word on the street is if you deal with Anthony Luca, you'll never get ripped off. Conversely, if you rip off Anthony Luca, you'll never deal again anywhere. Not in this life.

The word on the street is very important in that business, especially for a guy like my dad, who isn't famous at all outside his own circle. He keeps a pretty low profile. Most of the kids at school have no idea that my family is The Family. The only time Dad even made the papers was after the famous gangland assassination of Mario Calabrese in 1993. The cops are sure that my father ordered the hit, but they were never able to pin it on him. They just assumed he did it because, with Calabrese out of the picture, Dad was able to take over as the vending-machine king of New York. Dad won't say anything about it one way or the other, not even to Tommy, who joined him in the business shortly after that.

It didn't take very long for Tommy to develop a reputation just the opposite of my dad's. Tommy's loud, crude, and rough, with a temper like a cherry bomb. When the doorbell rings, he's the last guy you want to see standing there, except maybe Uncle Pampers.

Tommy has plenty of enthusiasm for his job. Maybe too much, as Jimmy Rat could tell you. So Dad brought over one of his top young guys and made him Tommy's partner. *Keeper* would be a better word.

Ray Francione used to be in charge of loan-sharking on Long Island's North Shore. If he's upset about being reassigned as nursemaid to a hothead, it doesn't show.

He isn't one of the uncles. I guess he technically counts as a cousin, although we're not related. I kind of wish we were. Of all the guys who work for my dad, I like Ray the best. He's such an awesome person that every now and then I have to stop and remind myself that he's a criminal.

When I get arrested because my sixteenth birthday present turns out to be hot, the uncles think it's the funniest thing that ever happened. Tommy's all for letting me spend the night in jail. Wiseguys can't seem to understand that there's a whole world out there that has nothing to do with The Life. But not Ray. When the uncles look at me like some exotic species of Gila monster because I'm passing up the chance to work with my father, Ray never judges me.

Who do you think bails me out and takes me home that

awful night? And while Tommy and the uncles act like being hauled away in handcuffs is all in a day's work, Ray really understands what a terrible experience it is for me.

Even Dad doesn't think it's such a disaster. "Don't worry, Vince. We'll get you another car."

I lay down the law. No more stolen cars. I'll buy my own car and pay for it with my own money. They don't yell at me, exactly. But they look as if I'm suggesting that we barbecue Mom on a rotating spit.

"But, Vince!" Tommy protests. "Do you have any idea the kind of lousy piece of crap you can afford?"

"Maybe. But it'll be mine. And nobody's going to take it away from me and use words like *grand theft auto.*"

Ray sticks up for me, even with Dad there. Not a lot of people have the guts to do that. And a week later, he finds a friend of a friend of a friend, who just so happens to have a nice little Mazda Protegé with only forty thousand miles on it.

I'm so proud of myself. "I can't believe I'm getting it for three thousand bucks!"

"You're not," says Ray. "Listen, you didn't hear it from me, but your father slipped me a few grand to make sure you get something decent."

I blow up. Poor Ray. Bad enough he has Tommy to deal with; now Anthony Luca's other son is going crazy on him.

But he's patient. "Take the money. He's your father. Let him help you out."

"I don't want to touch anything from my father's business."

He looks me squarely in the eye. "Your whole life is paid for by your father's business. The clothes on your back, the bed you sleep in at night, your mother's great cooking. Your father's business is the reason you can afford to stand here and be so high and mighty about your father's business. So, as we say in your father's business, forget about it."

Obviously, I buy the car.

My father always has a special smile when he sees my Mazda, even though it looks pretty lame next to the parade of limos and Beamers and Mercedes that are always coming and going at our place. Ray says Dad still disapproves of the way I got it—you know, legitimately.

But maybe that's what he likes about it—that his younger son did something he disapproves of.

[THREE]

WHEN **A**LEX STARTS NAGGING for something, it's usually a good idea to just suck it up and do what he wants. You'll save yourself a lot of grief. Because eventually, you're going to end up doing it anyway, just to shut him up.

That's why we go out for football that September—not for the competition or the glory, not for the exercise, not for the love of the game—but because, "Chicks can't resist shoulder pads."

Of all the cockamamie schemes in pursuit of Alex's Holy Grail, this is by far the cockamamiest.

Football tryouts are like marines training. Why countless hours of jumping jacks are required to prepare for a game that takes place in five-second bursts of activity, I'll never know. But when the dust clears after three rounds of cuts, we're still there. I manage to win a spot as the fourth-string halfback. And skinny Alex turns out to be a pretty fair kicker. We're proud shoulder-pad-wearing members of the Jefferson Jaguars.

"I hear those football parties are *wild!*" cheers Alex.

Either there are no football parties, or benchwarmers aren't invited. Our social lives still consist of each other.

Practice lasts a hundred hours a day. We have double workouts until our first game—an hour in the morning, just to get the blood pumping, and a ninety-minute marathon after school.

"Hang in there," Alex promises. "The rewards'll come. I know it. I can taste it."

"All I taste is sweat," I say sourly. "We're up at the crack of dawn; we don't get home till dinner, which is a two-hour stuffing festival at my house. Then I've got homework to worry about. Every girl in Nassau County could be after my aching bod, and I wouldn't have time to do anything about it."

Alex shrugs. "The other guys manage it."

"The other guys are signed up for Basket Weaving 101. We've got real courses, SATs to get ready for. That New Media class—I took it because I thought it was watching television. It's all about the Internet! We're going to have to design Web sites!"

"Yeah, I'm a little worried about that one too," Alex agrees. "Have you seen what a bunch of dweebs are in there? Girls could get the wrong idea about us."

"We'll wear our shoulder pads," I say sarcastically. "That'll fool them."

Our home opener is on Saturday. It's Alex's first chance to check out the cheerleaders, so he misses the whole warm-up and gets benched by Coach Bronski. With me being on the bench anyway, we sit together, watching other guys living the quintessential American high-school experience. Boy, going out for football has really changed our lives.

Our opponents are the Lions from Central High in Valley Stream. Neither team is very good, and it shows. The game is a huge yawn, destined to go into halftime at 0–0. I mean, even the cheerleaders are pretty listless. I see newspapers opened up in the stands. It's pathetic.

Coach Bronski is trying everything to get a little offense going. Eventually, he scrapes the bottom of the barrel, because I get a tap on one of the shoulder pads that make me so irresistible to women.

It's a run off the right tackle, and the second I touch the ball, I know the play is going nowhere. My blockers haven't cleared me an inch of space. All I can do is run into a bunch of fat behinds, theirs and ours. So there I am, surrounded by five defenders, and I brace myself for the big hit. It doesn't come. Maybe they don't realize I've got the ball. I push through and still nobody lays a hand on me. Finally, someone grabs the back of my jersey and gives a gentle pull. It's not much of a tackle, but I trip anyway, and down I go. I gain eight yards, which is the biggest offensive play by either team all day.

Coach leaves me in. I take a little pass. When I catch it, there's a linebacker right there to hammer me. The face looks kind of familiar, but I can't place it. And when I turn back again, he's gone! I start downfield. I don't know where the other team went, but they're sure not in front of me. Every inch of my forty-yard scamper to pay dirt, I'm expecting to get viciously hauled down from behind. It never happens.

Suddenly, our comatose fans are going nuts. The cheer-leaders are craning their necks, trying to read the name on my shirt so they can come up with a cheer for me. Somebody obviously needs glasses, because the cheer comes out, "Here we go, Lucy! Here we go!" *Stomp! Stomp!*

As I'm jogging back to the bench, I get a congratulatory slap on the butt. It's that linebacker from the other team, the one who didn't make the tackle.

He says, "Hey, Vince, remember me from Enza's wedding?"

That's how I know the guy! Johnny Somebody. His dad is Rafael, a member of Uncle Uncle's crew, out by JFK Airport. Sure we were at his cousin's wedding. Being the top dog, my father gets invited to every baptism, sweet sixteen, and yes, bar mitzvah. These days the vending-machine business crosses all ethnic boundaries.

On the bench, Alex looks almost resentful. "You didn't tell me you were *good.*"

I defend myself. "It was a fluke. Honest."

Pretty soon we get the ball back, and guess who gets sent in to rack up some more yardage? As I take my place in the backfield, the Lions' defense is looking at me with fear in their eyes. I'm a little confused, but it feels good. This is what it's like to be a star athlete. And I'm just getting started. Maybe I'm a natural.

Then I hear it, just a whisper from somewhere behind the line: *"That's him. Luca's kid."*

The wind comes out of my sails so fast that I'm dead in the

water. Superstar. Natural. Yeah, right. These guys won't lay a hand on me because Johnny blabbed about who my dad is. They think if they tackle me, and somehow I get hurt, Dad'll send Uncle Pampers over to pay them a visit.

I get the ball on every snap. A lot of arms reach for me, but nobody makes much contact. It's embarrassing! Eventually, I start falling down when I think someone *should* have made a tackle. But I can't play offense and defense at the same time. Pretty soon I've got another touchdown.

Back on the bench, I'm fuming. Of all the ways my dad's business screws up my life, this is the most insidious. I mean, Dad's not here. I made it a point to tell no one at home about the game. But he's here as surely as if he was sitting in the front row, threatening everybody.

It's crazy! Dad wouldn't care if someone tackled me. If I got hurt, he wouldn't blame it on anybody. It's like his absence speaks even louder than his presence. It's not his fault, but in a way it is. If he was a lawyer, or a cop, or a teacher, like other fathers—I'll bet *their* kids get tackled.

I can't even play football because of who I am. I set aside the fact that I don't really want to play football anyway, and decide to be mad about it.

I turn to Coach Bronski when we take possession again. "I don't want to go in on the next series."

He gapes at me, astonished. "You're eatin' them alive, Luca!"

"I can't explain right now, Coach," I plead, "but you've got to bench me!"

"Fat chance!" he roars. "Get out there!"

What can I do? I quit the team.

Alex shoots me a look, as if I just folded a royal flush in the World Poker Championships.

"I'll tell you about it later," I mutter, and head for the locker room.

"Hey, wait up! Hey, Vincent!"

I turn around. "It's Vince."

I've seen this girl at school. Honey-blond, petite. Pretty cute.

"I'm Kendra. Kendra Bightly. I'm covering the game for the *Jefferson Journal.*"

You can guess that, in my house, reporters are almost as popular as cops. Secrecy is very important in the vending-machine business. On the other hand, I'm not sure that extends to our school newspaper because nobody actually reads it.

"You're *missing* the game," I point out.

"I'm gambling that you quitting the team is the real story," she says seriously. "Want to talk about it?"

"God, no."

She doesn't go away. "You had a fight with Coach Bronski."

"Not really."

"Well, that's what I saw, so that's what I have to print. Unless," she adds, "you want to tell your side of the story."

I trudge into the locker room. She doesn't stop at the door. "Who wants to read about a fourth-string halfback?" I ask her.

Her face is so completely clueless that I realize she doesn't know what a fourth-string halfback is. She probably doesn't know a football from third base. Back in sophomore year, Alex tried to write for the *Journal.* His first assignment was to cover a dog show—the guy's so allergic he couldn't even breathe in the building. It must be some kind of hazing thing they do for the new reporters—sending them on a story they don't have a prayer of pulling off.

"You don't know anything about football," I accuse her. "So you've decided to write about the guy who quit the team."

Her expression remains tough, but a slight flush starts from under her collar and works its way up her neck to her cheeks. I'm not sure why, but something my mother told me pops into my head: *The problem with the young girls these days—they don't blush anymore.* I make a mental note to tell her she's wrong.

Then I say, "I'm supposed to get changed now."

Part of me just wants to watch her face turn from pink to crimson. But she's out of there before I get a chance to see it.

[FOUR]

MY TEACHERS DON'T HAVE VERY MUCH in common with my
father, but there is one thing they all share: everybody agrees
that I don't work hard enough. *Vincent has the potential to be
an excellent student if only he'd apply himself:* it's on every report
card I've gotten since kindergarten. So when Dad gave me
that whole lecture about getting motivated, he was just the
latest singer of an old song I'd been hearing for most of my
life. Teachers: *Get motivated about school;* Dad: *Get motivated
about the future;* Mom: *Get motivated about family;* Alex: *Get
motivated about girls.*

What can I say? It's not me. While a lot of seniors spend
their weekends filling out college applications, strategizing
about Ivy League schools, and second-choice schools, and
fallback schools, I've been letting all that slide. It's not that
I've got better things to do—God knows I've hung up my
shoulder pads. I just don't care that much.

Dad goes ballistic over this. "You could be the first Luca
to go to university!"

Never *college;* college is where Mira went. Harvard, Yale—*that's* university. Privately, I think he shouldn't hold his breath. The only way I'm getting into Harvard is if Dad sends one of the uncles to have a little talk with the dean of admissions. I'm not a straight-A student—at least not since fourth grade, when the Calabrese hit was big news. Back then some of my teachers put two and two together and figured out that I was related to the prime suspect. There was this one art teacher—when my dad showed up to take me to a dentist's appointment, she *ate* a piece of clay. She had been demonstrating how to make handles for ceramic pottery and she got so rattled that she just popped the clay into her mouth like chocolate. She wouldn't spit it out in front of Dad either. She swallowed it. Missed two days of school due to a "stomach virus."

But no one remembers the Calabrese murder anymore. And even if they do, they've certainly forgotten the guy the cops couldn't pin it on. Thank God. Life in the Luca house is tough enough without CNN camping on the front curb.

Actually, I wouldn't mind a little of that old notoriety for New Media class. Mr. Mullinicks is the toughest teacher in school. I'm not sure if he knows about my family, but I doubt that would change anything. He'd flunk me. He'd flunk Al Capone, and pack him off to summer school to make up the credits. And if Big Al put up a stink, Mr. Mullinicks would use his trademark line, "That's *your* problem."

"What should our Web sites be about?" asks a girl in the front row.

"That's your problem," Mr. Mullinicks informs her. "So

long as it's not obscene and nobody is trying to overthrow the government. And it's your problem to register your site with all the different search engines so you'll attract as much traffic as possible. Your grade will be based on one thing and one thing only—how many hits you can generate by the end of the semester."

Alex raises his hand. "What if you put together a great site, but not that many people find out about it?"

"That's your problem," the teacher tells him. "If a tree falls in the forest and nobody's there to hear it, does it make a noise? This class isn't about having a magnificent tree; it's about making a big noise. The challenge of the Internet is to reach customers in an increasingly crowded marketplace." He scowls at us. "And don't think you can have your grandmother logging on day and night. I expect to see hundreds of hits. How you accomplish that," he finishes, "is your problem."

"It must be nice to be Mr. Mullinicks," I say to Alex after class. "Everything is someone else's problem. I'd love to farm out all my problems and lead a trouble-free life."

Alex is distracted. "What are you wearing tonight?"

He's talking about Alfie Heller's party in the city. Alfie was at Jefferson last year. Now he's a freshman at NYU, and he's gotten the whole senior class invited to his fraternity's big bash—at least Alfie's friends, which means pretty much everybody.

There's a lot of buzz about it in the school halls. Going to a college party is every high-school kid's dream. A normal person would be psyched. A superconcentrated mass of hormones like Alex is vibrating like a guitar string.

"I'll wear *clothes*," I say. "Whatever I grab out of my closet. Come on, man, this party's supposed to be fun. Don't turn it into a chess match."

"There are going to be *college* girls there, Vince," he insists. "We can't get cocky about this."

"Oh, yeah, we don't want all the success we've had with high-school girls to go to our heads."

He's testy. "I can't think with all your negativity bouncing around my skull. Now, what do college girls like?"

"I'm guessing they're not too fond of an idiot who plans his wardrobe like D-day. When I get there, I'd better not see you stressing out."

"When you get there?" He's horrified. "You mean we're not going together?"

"I promised Tommy I'd drop by his apartment before the party." Tommy has a place in Greenwich Village, not far from NYU, although Mom keeps his room as if he never moved away. Part of her will never accept that he has.

"A single boy should live with his family until he gets married," she always says. It's not really that she misses Tommy, because he's home practically every day for business. She just has this fifties TV view of what a family should be. Mira married her high-school sweetheart, and Tommy and I are required to be Wally and the Beaver. This casts Anthony Luca as Ward Cleaver. The mind boggles. I could never get a handle on why this is so important to her until I first read *Hamlet* my junior year: "The lady doth protest too much, methinks."

Alex is distraught. "Why does it have to be *tonight*?"

I shrug. "He feels bad about the Angela O'Bannon disaster, and he wants to make it up to me. I think he's taking me out to dinner or something. We have to do that in secret or Mom thinks we're dissing her cooking. Anyway, I figured since I'm going to be in the city for this party—"

"You decided to blow me off at the most crucial moment of our love lives," he finishes.

"We don't have love lives," I remind him. "Don't worry, I'll be right by your side for every humiliating strikeout. Just try to hold off on embarrassing yourself until I get there, okay?"

No one in my father's business pays for parking. Ever. They just leave their cars any old place—expired meters, school crossings, next to hydrants. They get piles of tickets, and they don't pay those either. Tommy is *proud* of his. It's like the organized-crime version of collecting stamps—*Hey, I'll trade you* an *expired meter in Brooklyn for* a *Port Authority bus-loading violation.*

The amazing thing is I can't ever remember anybody getting in trouble for it. It's hard to explain, but look at it this way. When normal, law-abiding Joe Shmoe does something illegal, he gets caught. But people who live entire lives *outside* the law are somehow immune, as if the criminal code doesn't even apply to them. How could you get tripped up by something that's as alien and irrelevant to you as the ancient Egyptian Book of the Dead?

Moral of the story: If you're considering breaking a law, break all of them.

Great lesson, huh? Mobsters, like Charles Barkley, are not role models.

Since I'm a civilian, I aim the Mazda straight for the garage. Thirty bucks for the privilege of parking under Tommy's high-rise. Expensive, sure, but it seems appropriate for the only Luca who paid for his car using actual money.

Tommy's astronomical rent leases a smallish one-bedroom apartment on the twenty-third floor of a luxury doorman building. In the elevator I'm hoping he doesn't have anything too fancy planned. I'm wearing jeans and a short-sleeved button-down shirt. It's late September, and the days are still hitting seventy-plus.

I ring the bell of suite 23B.

"Hang on," calls a voice. Definitely not Tommy's.

How do I describe the individual who answers the door? Not stunning exactly, but *hot*. You know how supermodels are gorgeous, but there's an unnatural perfection to them? Well, this girl is about as good-looking you can get and still be a real person. She's a little younger than Tommy—early twenties, I'd guess. She's dressed casually, but her sexiness packs an atmospheric wallop like walking from air-conditioning into a hundred-degree day. Her sweater almost but not quite reaches the waistline of her low-rise jeans, revealing infinity sit-ups' worth of rock-hard abs. Words fail me, except these two: *Oh, my*.

She holds out her hand. "I'm Cece. You must be Vince."

I shake it, surprised but not blown away. Tommy runs with a fast crowd—okay, Tommy *is* a fast crowd. He has been known to date some pretty impressive women.

"Where's Tommy?" I manage.

"He told me to look after you till he gets back," she says airily. "Want a beer?"

"Coke's fine," I reply. "Driving."

"Coming up."

I can't help but watch her as she heads for the galley kitchen. I don't even try to look away. It's that kind of attraction.

I sit. She stands behind my chair, asking politely interested questions about me. If she doesn't care—and, let's face it, why should a twenty-something knockout want to hear about what courses I'm taking?—she doesn't show it. That's class. Tommy has latched onto a real keeper here.

That thought has barely crossed my mind when she starts massaging my shoulders. She's so smooth that it takes a second to realize that this isn't the most natural thing in the world.

"Where did you say Tommy was?"

She doesn't stop. "Oh, just taking care of a few things."

The last time Tommy took care of a few things, I ended up with Jimmy Rat in the trunk of my car. I start to tell Cece this, but now her hands are off my shoulders and she's rubbing my *chest*!

This is not good! I mean, it's *good*—it's *great*, actually. But not with Tommy's girlfriend. What the *hell* is she thinking?

"Uh—uh—Miss?"

"Cece."

Exactly when did her mouth get so close to my ear? I can feel the vibrations of her reedy voice in my pancreas, not to mention other places. Oh, this is *so* not good!

"Well—it's just that—uh—" Forget it. I'm jelly. No, worse. I'm a puddle of low-fat milk. "You know—uh—Tommy could walk in here any minute."

"Relax," she soothes, expertly springing the buttons of my shirt. "We've got a couple of hours."

"But—aren't you afraid he'll find out?"

"Silly," she laughs. "He already knows."

"He *does?*"

"Of course! Who do you think set this up?"

I have these moments—vending-machine moments. It's at these times when I come to understand that something I assumed was relatively innocent is actually part of Dad's world. Cece isn't Tommy's latest squeeze; she's a call girl! My brother brought me to his apartment so he could set me up with a *hooker*! *That's* his little gift to make up for the Jimmy Rat thing!

The realization is like a jolt of electricity applied simultaneously to every single cell in my body. I leap out of the chair, shirttails flapping like a flag. She's got her sweater half off, an image that will forever remain burned onto the back of my retinas. But I'm already running for the door.

Cece twigs to what's going on. "Hey," she says softly, the yellow cotton knit bunched around her shoulders. "It's okay to be scared if it's your first time."

"That's not it—" I babble.

But how could I ever explain it? The problem is where this little gift is coming from. I mean, your first time is pretty important, right? You carry it with you forever. I refuse to put the permanent stamp of organized crime on my love life.

On my wedding night, I shouldn't be thinking . . . *and it all started back in 2002 when Tommy used his Mob connections to hire me a call girl.* . . .

The sweater comes off the rest of the way. If I was a pinball machine, my response would be: *Tilt.* Cece speaks just one more word: "Stay."

There are encyclopedias that say less. In that single syllable, I can envision the next couple of hours, and they're rated NC-17.

I can't take my eyes off her, and I'm equally entranced and bewildered by the fact that in a few minutes, I'll be seeing a whole lot more. *Going all the way.* It sinks in that there's a set limit to how far you can go. It's not like long jump where you can train really hard and squeeze out another centimeter next time. This is the end. The max. The finish line. Will it be here and now for me?

Sensing the kill, Cece reaches for the clasp of her bra.

It's the toughest decision I've ever had to make, but I make it.

I'm out of there.

[FIVE]

ALEX ISN'T AS SUPPORTIVE AS a best friend should be.

"You *idiot*! You *moron*! You stupid brainless *dolt*!"

He's waiting for me outside the loft building that houses Gamma Kappa and a few other NYU frats.

"She was a call girl."

"That's even worse!" he howls. "You had guaranteed action and you blew it."

"I didn't blow it. I walked away. I don't take anything from my father's business."

"But can't you make an exception for *this*?"

"*This* goes double. When I think back to my first time, it's going to be something real, not something bought and paid for."

That gives Alex an idea. "If she's getting paid anyway, maybe I could head over there and go in your place."

"Don't give me that," I scoff. "You couldn't do it either."

He looks pained. "I know. I just can't stand to see it go to waste. It's like you're starving, but there's this beautiful twelve-course dinner prepared by the top chefs of Europe, and you have to say, 'No, thanks.'"

I award him a friendly slap on the back. "We're not starving. We just haven't been invited to the table yet. Come on, let's go to college."

It's called Fraternity Row, but it's really more like a column—six frat houses in lofts, one on top of the other. The building is a hundred and fifty years old, and looks twice that, with an elevator from the Jurassic period. As we rattle and shake toward Gamma Kappa on the fourth floor, I become aware of a new vibration—the pounding beat of dance music, steadily increasing in volume.

The doors shudder open and the blasting sound washes over us. I don't know what I expected a frat house to look like, but this is basically a large, unfinished space, empty of everything except people. There are hundreds of those, crammed in shoulder to shoulder. The smell of beer, smoke, and sweat is all pervading. And hot—imagine Death Valley, only a lot louder. You can't hear yourself think.

Alex looks around reverently. "This is it, Vince!" He has to shout it directly into my ear. "The promised land!"

Leave it to Alex to look at a riot and see perfection. If my old-fashioned Catholic mother caught a glimpse of this, she'd lock me in the house and fill me full of so much gnocchi I couldn't get up off the couch, let alone visit a den of iniquity. It's fine for sin to pay the bills, so long as I'm squeaky clean. No wonder Tommy hit the bricks.

I count at least seven or eight kegs around the room, and the floor is covered with a thin beery slime. The drinking is unreal—some of these kids are so smashed that it takes two or three friends to drag them to the nearest tap for a refill. The dancing is pretty crazy too, although motion is limited by the crush of people. A few try to throw their arms and legs around a little, but after kicking and punching their neighbors, they make so many enemies so fast that they're quick to mellow out. The smart guys grab their dates and hang on—and not just to avoid getting decked with a flying elbow. There's so much sexual tension in the air that you could lose your girlfriend between the hallway and the bathroom.

"Do you see anybody from Jefferson?" I call to Alex.

I'm not sure he hears. "This makes those football parties look like quilting bees!" he raves.

How would we know? I want to ask. But I'm saving my voice just in case I need it later to, let's say, communicate with the 911 operator.

We decide to split up to "check out the scene," as Alex puts it.

So I take a little tour, squeezing myself in between partygoers, lubricated by beer and perspiration. I see a few kids from school, but not as many as I expected. Suburban wimps! They talk a good game, but when it comes time to go into the big bad city, where are they? I feel a surge of pride for Alex, who I'm so rarely proud of. Even when his ride dropped out, he had the guts to get on that commuter train. Then again, Alex wouldn't miss this if he had to travel via the South Pole by dogsled.

As I pass a keg, a plastic cup of beer is forced into my

hand. I try to say no, but the kid at the tap won't take it back. "No man! You gotta drink it! You *gotta!*"

Even though he's standing in one place, he's wobbling. His eyes are little more than slits. To him it's perfectly logical: he's trashed, therefore everybody else has to be too. I love college. It's so much more mature than high school.

"Thanks," I mumble. As I'm searching for a place to set it down, a high-pitched voice cries out my name. Before I know it, some girl yanks me through the crowd and puts her arm around me!

I'm amazed. Who knows me in college—especially a cute girl? But then I recognize her. It's Kendra Bightly, that reporter from the *Jefferson Journal.* I'm kind of amazed she's even talking to me after I kicked her out of the locker room last weekend.

Then I see there's someone with her, hanging all over her, in fact—a college guy in khaki shorts and a beer-soaked Gamma Kappa T-shirt.

"Randy," she shouts over the din, "meet my boyfriend, Vince."

Boyfriend? Then I clue in. No wonder Kendra is so glad to see me. She'd be glad to see Jack the Ripper—anybody who could save her from this frat glork.

Randy holds out his hand, and I shake it. He's suspicious. "So, how long have you guys been going out?"

I can't resist. "Oh, years. Since middle school."

Skepticism. "Yeah?"

"Sixth-grade sweethearts," I assure him.

Frat boy's not suspicious anymore. He's just mad. For a

second I'm afraid he's going to take a swing at me. But no, he's just a sleazy college kid who thought he could impress a high-school girl with his mighty Gamma Kappa-ness. He's not going to fight. In fact, he's already scouting around for his next victim.

I hold Kendra's hand. She's looking at me as if I've just escaped from a mental institution. But she's got no choice; she has to take what I'm giving.

"I'll never forget the night we met," I continue romantically. "It was the science fair. There was perfume in the air—or was it formaldehyde?"

"Morons!" Randy snorts, and melts away into the crowd.

Kendra pulls free and belts me. It doesn't hurt, but the top third of my beer spills on my shoes.

"Hey!" I protest. "I *helped* you!"

"You didn't have to be such a jerk about it!"

"There was only one thing that would get rid of that frat boy," I argue. "And he's gone. You're welcome."

She's pretty upset. "College!" she snorts. "I can't wait!"

Suddenly, I want my beer. I take a sip and it tastes good in a gassy, bitter way. I don't know much about Kendra Bightly, but I can tell that this is not her element. It's not mine, either, but compared with her, I'm an honorary Gamma Kappa. She's lost in this smoky, pulsing sardine can.

"You didn't come alone, did you?" I ask.

"I took the train with a couple of friends. They're—" She gestures at the crush all around us. "They love this. Is it just me?"

I catch sight of Alex, stalking around the crowd, examining the goods like a kid in a candy store. "It's not just you," I say kindly.

"Seriously, are these the choices for a social life? Be a hermit or *this*?"

"My brother Tommy suggested a third way," I put in sardonically. "I won't bore you with the details."

Strange as it may seem, I feel an oblique connection with Kendra. She's as out of place at this party as I am in the Luca family. Take tonight. In a million years, you could never explain to Tommy that setting up a seventeen-year-old with a hooker isn't the world's most thoughtful present.

That's part and parcel of the Mob. Lawyers go home at night and stop being lawyers. But the vending-machine business is twenty-four/seven. They even call it The Life. Dad and Tommy don't work at their jobs; they *live* them. No wonder they can't keep me out of it.

And it doesn't help that they don't even see what they're doing to me. Once, just once, I'd like to hand it back to them in spades.

Yeah, right. I sigh and have another swig. Kendra stares at me with open distaste. My first thought is, Who cares what she thinks? But there's another part of me—the part trained by Mom about not being rude.

"Can I get you something? There's beer and"—I glance around—"beer."

She looks twice as uncomfortable as before. "That would be perfect. I can just see the headline: FBI Agent's Daughter Snagged in Underage-Drinking Sting Operation."

There's an attention getter. "Your dad works for the FBI?"

She nods, and I realize that it's hanging right out there in front of me. The only way I could ever give my family the equivalent of a vending-machine moment.

It's as if an unseen force takes over, and I have absolutely no say in the matter. I grab Kendra by the shoulders and kiss her.

I don't know—I still can't explain it. But I'm really not expecting what happens next. She's rigid for a second, and then she relaxes and kisses me back. I reflect that the history of my love life is pretty pathetic. I wasted my first make-out worrying about the body in my trunk, and here's number two coming off a near miss with a call girl, when the only thought in my head is "In your face, Dad, I'm kissing the FBI!" Dancers jostle us, full-to-overflowing beers whiz by our heads, but we don't come up for air for a long time.

Somewhere, a fight breaks out. Fists fly. I feel rather than hear the impact of knuckles on somebody's chin. The victim hurtles through the crush, bursting right between Kendra and me. The guy hits the floor in a shower of beer slop and bounces right up again, eager for battle. Instantly, three peacemakers materialize. The kid's so mad that, in order to keep him from charging, the three have to drive him back, plowing through the crowd. Somehow, I get caught up in this wedge, stuck between the fighter and his buddies. The string of curses he spews right into my face would make Tommy blush, and, trust me, Dad's business isn't exactly high tea at Buckingham Palace. There are angry shouts and screams as we bull right through a pack of dancers.

It all fizzles out soon enough, but when I make my way back to Kendra, she's gone. Frowning, I look around, navigating by the posters on the walls. She was definitely at the intersection of the Notre Dame football pennant and Miss February 1999. What happened?

Searching for a five-foot-two girl at a packed frat party is like trying to track down a lost Chihuahua in a mature cornfield. For the next hour, I push through every square inch of that loft, becoming more desperate with each passing minute. This is worse than the Angela O'Bannon thing. At least there was a tangible reason why things didn't work out with Angela. This makes no sense at all.

Eventually, I stake out the ladies' bathroom. The free flowing of eight kegs has turned this narrow stretch of hallway into the most popular real estate in Gamma Kappa House. I think every coed at NYU squeezes by, tossing all manner of dirty looks in my direction, and I pick up the occasional murmured "Pervert!" I can't even blame them. What kind of a deviant positions himself like a sentry outside the ladies' can?

"Hey, Vince!" comes a voice. "Over here!"

It's Alex, just a few feet—but several people—away from me. We're the only two guys in the area.

"I'm trying to find someone!" I call back to him.

"Tell me about it!" He leans over to talk into my ear. "But it's useless. College girls are so into themselves. This party sucks."

So much for the Promised Land. I make an executive decision. "Let's get out of here."

As we push back to the main loft, who do we run into but Randy, the frat glork.

"Hey, loser!" he jeers. "I saw your *girlfriend*! She just walked out with two of her friends!" And he dumps a full pitcher of beer over my head and dances away, laughing.

From this entire exchange, Alex jumps on a single factoid. "Girlfriend?!"

"He's talking about Kendra Bightly!" I say in self-defense, teeth chattering. The beer is ice cold, and I'm soaked to the skin. "That reporter!"

"But why does that guy think she's your *girlfriend*?" he persists.

I've had it. Dripping beer, I start to plow through the crowd toward the exit. If Alex isn't ready to leave yet, that's his problem. He follows, spouting questions, which I ignore.

Near the door, I spy Alfie Heller, our NYU connection. He's got a beer in each hand, a girl on each arm, and, for some reason, a bowling trophy around his neck, hanging by a bike lock. Seeing us, he transfers the cups to the ladies, and pumps first my hand and then Alex's.

"Hey, guys, how's it going? Glad you could make it!"

If he notices that I look and smell like I've just taken a swim in the mighty Budweiser, he keeps it to himself.

I do my best to appear grateful. "Awesome party, Alfie. Thanks for inviting us."

"You're *leaving*?" He's appalled. "So soon? It's still empty!"

"Car's at a meter and I'm out of quarters," I lie.

He's all concern. "You're not *driving*? Dude, you reek like a brewery!"

"Just my hair and clothes," I sigh. Good point, though. I've only had a couple of sips, but if I happen to get pulled over on the way home, the cop will take a whiff and assume I've been drinking all night.

Back on the street, I give Alex the whole story about Kendra and me.

He's furious. "You blew it *again*? Vince, you're killing me! This is my love life we're talking about."

"It was a one-in-a-million thing," I argue. "That atmosphere brings out the craziness in people. We're lucky there weren't any ax murderers at the party."

We ransom the car out of the garage and head home. At Alex's house, I take a shower while we wash my shirt and jeans. It's late, but the vending-machine business never closes, and Dad could easily be up with some of the uncles. My father has zero tolerance for drinking and driving, possibly because it's the only vice he doesn't get a cut of. Of course, I haven't *really* been drinking, but Dad doesn't know that, and with my hair and clothes soaked with beer, it's not worth the hassle.

I finally roll into the driveway around one. Turns out Dad's up, but not for business reasons. He's waiting for me in the living room, sanding a lopsided salad bowl over a wastebasket.

"Tommy called. He told me about his little surprise for you. I want to make sure you're all right with what happened."

"I *thought* he was taking me out to dinner," I say feelingly.

He's patient. "He was only trying to get square. You

bust somebody's TV, it's on you to find him a new one."

"Nobody busted my—" It all comes together in my head. The Jimmy Rat incident cost me a chance with Angela O'Bannon, so Cece was there to supply me with what Angela hadn't. Unbelievable. Sex is no different from a television set in my father's business. A commodity—something to be traded, bought, sold.

"In your world, maybe," I say sharply. "Not mine."

Dad nods understandingly. "You're right, Vince. Your brother—sometimes I wonder whether he's got brains or coleslaw in there. But his heart—that's pure gold. You should have heard him on the phone. In his mind, he gave you the greatest present in the world. A lot of kids your age would have jumped at it."

"I was almost one of them," I admit.

Dad laughs. "But you weren't. You always have to do things your own way. I love that about you, Vince. A little crazy, but it's a sure sign that you'll succeed in business."

I shoot him a harsh look.

"In *any* business." He adds, "You're thinking about what you want to do, right?"

"Even in my sleep," I reply sarcastically.

He shakes his head. "You've got some mouth on you." He inspects the bowl. He's sanded a dime-sized hole in the bottom.

"Nice funnel."

"Smart guy." He drops bowl and sandpaper into the basket and turns to the lamp. "We're going to bed if that's okay with you, Agent Bite-Me." And he kills the light.

It's a good thing too, because I'm pretty sure I've just gone white to the ears.

Bite-Me—Bightly. Kendra Bightly, whose father works for the FBI.

"Vince, you coming?"

"Yeah, Dad." My heart is racing. Kendra's father isn't just *an* FBI agent; he's *our* FBI agent.

I just made out with the daughter of the man whose goal in life is to send my father to prison.

[SIX]

"YOU'VE GOT TO ASK HER OUT."

Alex has already said it seven times, and it isn't even lunch yet.

"Come on," he persists. "She's *into* you."

"It was a frat party," I reply between clenched teeth. "People do strange things—and I include myself in that."

We're in the library to research our Web sites for New Media. At least that's what we're supposed to be doing.

"Look, you blew it with Angela. You blew it with Cece. You've got to make something happen with Kendra. You owe it to me!"

"Even if she liked me—which she doesn't," I begin, "what am I supposed to do, invite her over? Her father has the place bugged, remember? I'm sure he'll be thrilled to hear his own daughter over his surveillance operation."

Alex shrugs. "She has a house."

"He *lives* there!" I explode.

"Not all day," Alex reasons. "Those guys put in big hours.

It's a lot of work investigating a major underworld kingpin."

I let that last comment pass. "Can we do this? We have to pick our topic today."

"Oh, I'm done," he informs me. "I've even registered my domain name."

He swivels his monitor to face me.

I stare at it. "MisterFerrariDriver? A Web site about Ferraris?"

"Chicks dig sports cars."

"But you drive a Ford Escort—when you can con your mom into lending it to you."

He's unfazed. "On the Internet I have a Ferrari. No, *two* Ferraris—a red one and a black one."

"You're going to flunk," I warn him. "Guys with Ferraris have better things to do than to sit in front of a computer downloading pictures of what's parked right outside in the driveway. If you want a successful Web site, you've got to appeal to the get-a-life crowd."

"Like who?"

"How about guys who go to Star Trek conventions?"

"*I* went to a Star Trek convention once!"

"And you're online a lot," I reason. "So are those people in the soap-opera chat rooms and the country-music fan pages. I'm not trying to insult you. I'm just saying that to have a successful Web site, you have to appeal to the kind of person who's on the Web. Think about what's going to attract the interest of old ladies who live alone with nineteen cats."

"You're delusional," he says accusingly, but I know I'm on to something.

I start checking domain names. *Cat* is taken, along with *catlover*, *mycat*, *catperson*, *lovemycat*, and *ilovemycat*. I start to fiddle around with the spelling and pretty soon I've registered my new site: ILuvMyCat.

If it's traffic Mr. Mullinicks wants, this should be rush hour in Manhattan. Not only are there zillions of cat owners out there, but judging by the number of cat sites, most of them like nothing better than talking about their pets.

Alex is unimpressed. "This is stupid, Vince. At least I *like* Ferraris. You can't stand cats."

"For one semester," I assure him, "I can fake it." Just to get his goat, I add, "And think how many girls out there must be cat lovers."

He's miffed that my idea is better than his. He looks at my head. "Hey, Vince, you know you've got dandruff?"

"Oops, sorry. I hope I don't get flakes all over the black leather upholstery in your Ferrari."

"No, seriously," he insists, brushing at my hair. "Get some Head and Shoulders, will you?"

Normally, I wouldn't give it a second thought. But for the last couple of days my head has been feeling kind of itchy. So when class is over, I find an out-of-the-way bathroom.

The light is terrible and the mirror is smeared with the kind of generic grime that only collects in public restrooms. I find a clear spot and sift through my 'do, separating the thick hair so I can see down to my scalp. He's right! Flakes!

And then a tiny piece of dandruff moves.

* * *

Nurse Jacinin switches off the light on the magnifying scope and swivels it back to the examining chair. "Head lice."

I'm blown away. "But I shower twice a day!"

She shrugs. "That doesn't do anything."

"It's impossible!" I persist. "My mother is a clean freak! I don't have any younger brothers or sisters! I never put on strange hats!"

I make her prove it to me. Big mistake. She finds an infested hair, yanks it out, and holds it under the scope. The sight turns my legs to jelly. My head is inhabited by a family of miniature white tarantulas. I am no longer aware of any itch. Now I feel pounding dinosaur tracks complete with clawed feet digging into my head.

"Oh, you can't feel lice," she says airily. "They're far too tiny. The discomfort you're experiencing is an allergic reaction on your scalp to the insects' feces."

Well, that makes me feel *so* much better. Not only has my cranium been colonized by tiny bugs, but they're also using me as an outdoor toilet.

Schools handle head lice the way people in the Middle Ages used to treat the Black Death. I'm banished for a minimum of twenty-four hours. During that time, I have to shampoo with this special lice-killing gunk. Even then I'm still banned until the nurse has inspected my head. And—get this—she has to do it *outside the building* before I'm allowed back in. Why don't they just spray-paint the word *UNCLEAN* across my chest?

"Touch no one as you exit the school," she orders, escorting me out of the examining room. "That goes for furniture as well. Lice and their larvae can live up to fifty-five hours on clothing and upholstery." The last part she belts out so that anyone within three football fields knows I've got cooties.

I'm still protesting. "But, Nurse Jacinin, I just don't understand how it's possible that I *got* the lice in the first—"

I fall silent. There, dead center in the row of sickos waiting to get in to see the nurse, sits Kendra Bightly. Her shoulder-length hair is tucked up inside a Yankees cap.

Well, that explains a lot. If butterflies can migrate all the way from Brazil, than I guess it's not too hard to accept that a truly motivated louse could walk down a strand of Kendra's hair and hop onto a strand of mine during a brief but memorable make-out session at a frat party.

Dad must have said it a million times: "Lousy FBI agents!" I never realized he was talking about their families' personal hygiene.

She ignores me, so I pretend I don't see her as I exit the nurse's office. But later, as I'm pulling out of the school parking lot—keeping my infested hair a few inches off the headrest; it's all I need to have to fumigate the Mazda on top of everything else—who do I see trudging to the local bus stop but Kendra.

My first thoughts are sympathetic. She's probably on her way to the pharmacy to pick up the same antilice treatment I have to get. With no car, it's going to take her three different buses to get to CVS.

A flush of anger. She's the one who gave me lice in the first place! And it's not like we have a long-term relationship. We made out—just once—in the middle of a drunken frat party.

Afterward she wouldn't even acknowledge that I was alive. For all I know, this Miss Innocent FBI Agent's Daughter stuff is just an act. Maybe she hops from guy to guy, spreading cooties like some head-lice Typhoid Mary.

I pull over in front of the bus stop and roll down the window. "Hi."

She looks as miserable as I feel. "Hi."

I take a deep breath. "I think we're going to the same place. Hop in."

"I don't know what you're talking about," she says stubbornly.

In the vending-machine business, I believe the appropriate line here would be: *You can either ride in the car or at the end of a rope behind it. Take your pick.*

Fortunately, I'm a civilian. "The drugstore," I explain patiently. "You know—to buy the special shampoo."

Avoiding my eyes, she gets in the car. The silence as we drive along is pretty uncomfortable. After all, what is there to say? *I'm infested; how about you?*

And finally, just as I'm parking outside CVS, she blurts, "I work in a day-care center."

"Oh—uh—that's nice—"

"That's where the lice are from," she explains. "There's an outbreak in the toddler room. I got it from the kids. And you got it when we . . ." Her voice trails off.

"Don't worry about it," I say gallantly. "It's not like it's incurable or anything like that."

Well, maybe it's curable, but the cure sure doesn't come cheap. We need Permethrin lice-eradicating hair treatment, a gel to loosen the eggs from the follicles, a fine-tooth Lice Meister nit comb, special shampoo made from tea tree oil, and even a spray insecticide for our clothes and pillows. The Permethrin alone costs thirty bucks.

Kendra rummages around her pocketbook. "Oh, no."

I check my wallet. Forty-three dollars—not enough for all this stuff, and definitely not enough to help her out. I've got a credit card for emergencies, but it's from my dad, and monetary instruments from him are not always one-hundred-percent legitimate. The name of the issuing bank doesn't exactly inspire confidence: Banco Commerciale de Tijuana. I don't know how much they'd appreciate their hard-earned pesos going to pay for my delousing.

"Maybe we can split it," she suggests shyly. "You know, buy just one set. I think we've got enough money for that."

"But—" A dozen logistical problems come to mind.

"My parents both work," she explains. "We'll be finished by the time they get home."

It comes to $61.40; we spring for an extra Lice Meister so we can each have one. We're supposed to comb for nits for two weeks.

Kendra lives in a subdivision of small, neat split-level homes at the far end of the attendance district for Jefferson. It's a nice neighborhood, but it's pretty obvious that FBI agents make a lot less money than the people they investigate. Le Château Luca has eight thousand square feet and a four-car garage, even though, according to DMV records, I am the only family member who actually owns a car.

It feels pretty weird to be in Agent Bite-Me's house. So

this is where the guy hangs out when he's not at work, listening to my family pass gas.

Upstairs, Kendra changes into an old jogging suit and tosses me a faded sweatshirt. "This is my dad's. See if it fits."

I pull it over my head and examine myself in the mirror. Across my chest it says FBI. Me, Vince Luca. This is like Captain Ahab in a SAVE THE WHALES T-shirt.

The process begins. We go down to the laundry room and take turns rubbing Permethrin into each other's hair. I figure this has to make me some kind of man of the world. I mean, I still have no love life, but I'll bet not even Casanova ever spent an afternoon massaging insecticide into a woman's scalp.

I won't try to build the suspense. The stuff is disgusting. It smells like embalming fluid, and it burns. I'm sure the poor lice suffer as they go, but not half as much as the owner of the head they're infesting.

That stays in for thirty minutes—already a longer stretch than I've ever spent with Kendra. It's kind of awkward. We have nothing in common except head lice. So we pass the time by spraying our clothes with the anti-egg stuff. Then we go upstairs and do her pillow, blanket, and sheets.

We're just about to head back to the basement to rinse the stuff out in the laundry sink when the front door opens and a voice calls, "Anybody home?"

Kendra's surprised. "Uh-oh, my dad. I didn't want him to know about this."

She doesn't want him to know about this? That goes quadruple for me! I mean, doesn't every FBI agent dream of the day that he gets home early and walks in on his daughter washing her hair in the company of a mobster's son?

"I've got to get out of here!"

"Don't I wish," Kendra agrees.

"No, really!" I look around. The window is the only way out, but the backyard is sloped, so there's a ten-foot drop to the ground.

I'm weighing the idea of two broken ankles when I spot it. The bedroom next door—the master—is located above a screened-in porch. I can get out onto the porch roof and climb down from there. I run into her parents' room.

Kendra follows me. "I was kidding. It's not the end of the world."

But I'm already climbing up on the night table to get to the window. My foot knocks over a tube of Preparation H, and I have an insane desire to laugh. It seems only fair that I know something embarrassing about Agent Bite-Me after he's been spying on my family all this time.

Footsteps on the stairs set my mind back to business. I jump the four-foot drop to the flat roof.

Kendra sticks her head out the window. "But we're not finished yet!"

"Save my half of the stuff," I call up to her. I roll to the edge, grab hold of the drainpipe, and heave myself over the side. The gutter comes away from the wall, and I crash painfully to the ground. And here I thought this kind of thing only happens in Adam Sandler movies.

The drainpipe now hangs away from the porch like a grotesquely reaching metal sculpture.

I consider trying to fix it, but then I hear Kendra's voice: "You're home early, Daddy."

I just run. With any luck, the guy isn't a very good FBI agent and won't lift my sneaker prints off his tube of Preparation H.

My racing heartbeat is back to normal by the time I turn into the driveway at home. I park and sneak in the side door. I have no desire to explain what's in my hair. Wouldn't you know it? Dad notices me just as I make for the stairs. But it isn't my hair that catches his eye.

"God, Vince, where'd you get that shirt?"

Heart sinking, I look down, already knowing what I'm going to find. I'm still wearing Agent Bite-Me's sweatshirt. My chest is a billboard for the FBI.

"That's priceless!" howls my father, helpless with laughter. "Can you get a couple for me and Tommy? Better yet, a bunch. Some of your uncles would drop dead over them!"

I mumble something about ordering an assortment from a novelty shop in the city and try to break away from him. But he gets a clean look at me, and probably a whiff, too.

"Jeez, Vince, when I was your age, I put grease in my hair, and that was bad enough. But you smell like a mortuary."

I don't argue the point. That's another thing there's a lot of in the vending-machine business: funerals.

[SEVEN]

Aʟʟ ᴛᴏʟᴅ, **I** ᴛʜɪɴᴋ ᴛʜᴇ **P**ᴇʀᴍᴇᴛʜʀɪɴ spends about seventy minutes in my hair, more than double the recommended maximum. The good news is that no louse could survive it. The bad news is not much of my scalp does either. By morning, I'm sore and flaking. My hair is still attached, thank God. But what I can see of the skin underneath is bright red. Even my split ends have split ends.

I'm not welcome at school, the twenty-four-hour ban is still in place. But rather than try to explain to Mom that her son—his head in particular—is "totally out of commission," I take my brown-bag lunch and drive away.

I cruise around for a while, idly calculating how many movies it'll take to get me to three thirty. I'm flush again—allowance from Dad. Just in the nick of time, too, since I blew all my cash on head-lice remedies. That's when it hits me: Kendra still owes me my half of the stuff we got at the drugstore. I doubt that any lice could have made it through the nuclear winter on my head, but the nurse said school rules require me to go through the full procedure.

I kill time until after nine and then head over to Kendra's through the thinning Long Island traffic. Just to be on the safe side, I park three blocks away from her house. I don't want Agent Bite-Me running my plates through the FBI computer. *A Luca is visiting our daughter! Oh, joy!* I don't think so.

Kendra's home alone except for the guys from Secure-O-Matic, who are installing a new burglar alarm.

"Daddy thought someone tried to break in off the porch roof yesterday," she explains with a nervous smile.

"There are a lot of wackos out there," I agree, poker-faced. "Good thing the FBI is on the job." I hand her a brown paper bag. "Your dad's shirt."

The alarm guys are snickering at us as we head for the basement. But trust me, it's all business. We rub egg-loosening gel on our heads, rinse it out in the laundry sink, and then comb each other with Lice Meisters. The teeth on those things are so fine that you need a hydraulic crane to pull them through your hair and a gag to muffle your screams. If you ever used a Lice Meister to make a kazoo, I'll bet only dogs could hear it.

She's the first one to bring up yesterday. "You know, you didn't have to play Spiderman out the window. My folks realize I'm not six years old anymore."

I try to make a joke out of it. "Hey, federal agents are armed."

She laughs. "I know he carries a gun, but I've never even seen it. He has a strict rule about keeping his work separate from his home life. I guess he rubs elbows with some pretty bad people."

Yeah, like my nearest and dearest.

I rush to change the subject. The Bightlys have a family room set up in the basement. "Nice stereo," I say, scanning shelves full of audio equipment. "Two stereos." Then I realize that the second speaker I'm staring at is hooked up to a microphone. "Is that a—karaoke machine?"

She's tight-lipped. "Yeah. So?"

The thought of Agent Bite-Me singing karaoke is even more mind-blowing than his hemorrhoids. I just can't wipe the huge grin off my face. "No, it's fine. It's just kind of hard to picture an FBI agent standing in his basement belting out 'You Are the Wind Beneath My Wings.'"

She won't even meet my gaze, and I can barely hear her mumble, "It's not his; it's mine."

Well, that's even weirder. This serious, straitlaced reporter from the school paper is a closet performer.

I'm genuinely interested. "Sing something," I encourage her. "No."

"Come on. I'll bet you're great."

"You're making fun of me."

"No," I say honestly. "I'm looking for a way to kill time until I can go home without having to tell my parents why I was kicked out of school today. Come on, I'll do it with you."

We compromise. I promise not to laugh, and she plays me a tape she made of her song stylings. I can't help noticing that she has racks of these cassettes, all marked with the semi-clever, semi-idiotic name *K-Bytes*.

She's good. She's great, actually. Her speaking voice is high and cutesy, but singing, she comes across deep and throaty—almost sexy. It's a very Alex way of thinking, but I'm kind of impressed that I made out with a girl who can sound like that.

I clap when the song ends, but she hits STOP and refuses to play me another one.

"Come on," I laugh. "You're awesome. I want to hear more."

She bops me on the head with the cassette case, and it actually hurts, what with my incinerated scalp and all. But I don't complain because I feel like something is different now. There's a subtle change in the atmosphere between us that's both scary and irresistible all at once.

I grab her around the shoulders and snatch the plastic box from her hand. "Now you're going to eat this," I growl.

"Make me," she snarls back.

But we both know we're not fighting, and whatever's going on has nothing to do with a cassette case.

By the time we start kissing, we're both really into it, and our session at the frat party seems like a half-speed workout with no tackling. We sink to the couch, breathing as if we've just run a mile.

It's almost like I'm two people. One of them is Marco Polo, determined to advance, explore, experience. The other is a real pain in the butt who can't stop thinking, This is Agent Bite-Me's daughter; this is Agent Bite-Me's house; this is Agent Bite-Me's couch.

I don't know who her two people are, but one of them

makes a small sound in the back of her throat. And it's not the perky speaking voice, either. It's the *singing* voice.

This is Agent Bite-Me's floor, the pain in the butt reminds me as we topple off the couch.

Shut up! snaps Marco Polo. By this time, he's really running the show.

Even I'm starting to wonder how far all this might go when the guys from Secure-O-Matic decide to test the new burglar alarm.

To say we hit the ceiling is to understate the matter. When we come back to earth, she's on one side of the basement, and I'm on the other. If I look as shocked as she does, we are one stunned pair. It's completely illogical, but the two of us are thinking the same thing—that we generated enough steam to set off the smoke detector.

Then the buzzer stops and a voice from upstairs calls, "Just a test. Sorry."

This is accompanied by strangled laughter.

I'm enraged, but I've got to hand it to those guys. They knew what we were heading downstairs to do before we did. I wouldn't hire them to alarm my house, but if I ever need a mind reader, I won't go to the lady with the tarot cards.

I can't remember a moment ever feeling so weighty with significance. The incident at the frat party could have been a fluke, but this is no fluke. The world is not the same place that it was when we woke up that morning.

She just says, "Wow," and I nod. But neither of us knows what comes next.

Kendra calls up the stairs to the Secure-O-Matic crew, "You guys are almost done, right?"

Prayer, the short-term kind at least, does me no good, because the reply comes back, "A few more hours to go, Miss." More laughing.

I'm ready to hang out all day waiting for them to leave, but Kendra has a story to write for the *Jefferson Journal*—an exposé on which teachers give out the most A's.

"They'll never let you print it," I predict.

She sighs. "Probably not. But I have to try. Teachers ramble on and on about freedom of the press, but God help you if you actually try to *use* it. Which reminds me—you never answered my question about why you quit the Jaguars."

Yikes. "Uh—you had it right the first time. Coach Bronski—the guy's a fascist." A silent apology to the coach, who's probably really nice.

"That took guts," she says admiringly. "I should do a follow-up piece—you know, about how hard it is to leave football for the courage of your convictions."

"It's okay. I'm using the extra time to concentrate on—other things." But at this moment, the only other thing I can think of is Kendra, and what just happened in her basement.

Leaving is awkward, and the presence of the two Secure-O-Matic technicians doesn't make it any more comfortable. Mostly, we talk lice business. I take my nit comb and my half of the tea-tree-oil shampoo. I get the spray too because my bedclothes haven't been done yet. And the way things seem to be going, the cooties could continue to commute back and forth between our heads. Believe it or not, the thought isn't entirely repulsive.

I take down her phone number but freeze when she asks for mine. Our lines are all bugged—by her own father, no less. How great would that be: Agent Bite-Me, hearing his sweet little daughter on the Luca tapes.

"We're getting a new number," I lie.

The investigative reporter in her looks suspicious.

"Crank calls," I explain quickly. "My mother's panicked."

Yeah. Mom's pretty helpless when she doesn't have a chicken potpie handy.

There's a kiss good-bye involved. It would be longer, but Secure-O-Matic sets off the alarm again. This time I know they did it on purpose.

From Kendra's house, I head straight for Ray Francione. When he's not with Tommy, Ray can usually be found at the Silver Slipper, a bar in Long Beach.

The guy at the door tells me to get lost. But then someone recognizes me, and I get the royal treatment.

"Vince!" Ray appears out of the back room, where I'm pretty sure a lot of vending-machine business goes on. "What's the problem? Why aren't you in school?"

I laugh. "You're Tommy's baby-sitter, not mine."

He turns pale. "Not so loud! People got big ears. If that gets back to your brother, there's going to be pain to go around." He pulls up a bar stool. "Why are you ditching class?"

I say stuff to Ray that I wouldn't even tell my own mother.

"Head lice. It's a twenty-four-hour pass. Listen, Ray, I need a big favor. Can you get me a cell phone that's untraceable to me?"

"Untraceable?" He's instantly alert. "If you're dealing drugs—"

"You know me better than that," I retort. "There's this girl, Ray—at least I think there is. I want to be able to talk to her without the FBI listening in."

Notice how I don't bore him with the details of who she is, and more important, who her father is. That's on a need-to-know basis, and nobody needs to know. I wish I didn't.

Ray nods understandingly. "I can probably come up with something."

"Today?"

"Relax, Romeo," he grins. "I just want to make sure you know what you're getting into. This is a cloned phone. It's illegal, right?"

"I'll pay for it," I insist. "I just don't want it to be bugged. If I went to the store and set up a real account, the FBI would be listening in by the end of the week."

Ray laughs. "You can't pay for it, dummy. What, you're going to send AT&T thirty bucks a month anonymously for a phone they don't even know exists?"

Good point. But I'm not really sweating the small stuff. Kendra has assumed a place in my brain where logic has no sway. "I still need it," I insist.

"It's yours," he assures me. "So long as you know what you're doing. You're the one who's always moaning and groaning about staying out of your father's business. This is part of it. This girl must really be something special."

I shrug helplessly. "I don't know. I've got nothing to compare it to. Maybe it's the stupidest thing I've ever done."

"Does she know who you are?"

I shudder. "God, no!"

He reaches out and ruffles my deloused hair. "You've got the right to be seventeen. Listen, your mind must be working a mile a minute right now. Just try to relax and enjoy it. It's never going to be this new again."

Ray's the best. He promises to drop by with the phone tonight.

As I leave the Silver Slipper, it occurs to me that seventeen years living under Anthony Luca's roof couldn't make a criminal out of me. *That* took half an hour in Kendra Bightly's basement.

On the way home, I swing by the grocery store and buy thirty dollars' worth of canned goods and cereals, which I take over to the food bank at St. Bartholomew. Call it a donation of my monthly cell phone fee from the Good Samaritans at AT&T.

[EIGHT]

KENDRA AND I CONTINUE TO SEE each other—if *see* is the right word. I take her to dark movie theaters; we spend our afternoons in the gloom of her basement, and evenings crammed into my parked Mazda. If Jimmy Rat thinks the trunk is too small, he should try to maneuver in the backseat.

We see each other in daylight too, but that's mostly at school, with Alex hanging around. Which is becoming a bit of a problem because he really, truly hates her.

It's nothing against Kendra. He would hate anyone in her position right now. I'm coming to see that all that blather about living his love life through me is exactly that, blather. He's just plain jealous, and I'd tell him so if it wasn't for the fact that I genuinely feel bad for the guy. He's languishing on the bench of that stupid football team, with not so much as a single date to show for countless hours of brutalizing practice. His shoulder pads are doing him about as much good as his virtual Ferraris. The one thing he had going for him was a best friend in exactly the same boat. We could while away our evenings and weekends plotting an end to our dweeb-hood. And now I'm with Kendra all the time, and he's high and dry. He doesn't admit this, of course. He pretends to be Kendra's best friend. To me he uses terms like "our girlfriend" and "our relationship."

It bugs me. "She's not 'our girlfriend.' She's not even *my* girlfriend, really. We just hang out."

"No," he says sternly. "You and I hang out. You and Kendra take care of business."

I'm heating up. "We don't 'take care of business.' Come to think of it, what the hell is taking care of business? Speak English!"

"You can call it whatever you like," he says smugly. "Just so long as I get all the details."

It's a sticky situation. Although no specific contract was ever signed, it was always assumed between Alex and me that each would tell the other anything that was going on vis-à-vis the fairer sex. Now that I've got something to share, I'm not sure I can do it. And instead of acting on a great surge of loyalty to Kendra, I basically feel like a welcher.

As usual, an experience that is pure bliss for most people ends up being just plain complicated for me. I'm juggling Alex with one hand while trying to navigate so that I never end up in the same room with Agent Bite-Me. Then there are the Lucas, who can't find out about this relationship either. It's nerve-racking!

The time with Kendra is great—almost too great. I've never been addicted to anything, thank God. So I couldn't imagine how you fall into a trap like that until I started dating Kendra. When I have to see her, I just *have* to, and I'm willing to jump through any number of hoops to get to her. I'd feel like a complete idiot except for the fact that she's the same way about me.

And it doesn't help that she's so busy. Kendra is one of those people whose schedule always has to be jam-packed. She works at the day-care center; she writes for the *Journal*; she takes advanced lifesaving at the Y; and she gives piano lessons to little kids on the side. There are CEOs with more leisure time!

Not wanting to seem like a loser, I pretend to have just as hectic a calendar. I invent a bunch of part-time jobs to explain why I always have money, in case Kendra's reporter's instincts or inherited FBI-agent DNA starts to question that. It sure beats telling her the truth, that underworld kingpins pay good allowance.

It's not a very good sham, but it works for now. In reality, you need motivation to be as busy as Kendra, and it's already been established by just about everybody that I don't have any. The one thing I'm motivated to do is hang out with Kendra. Sometimes the only way to do that is to drive her places. We use the transit time wisely, making out during red lights and while stuck in traffic. I take only the most congested routes. Soon I've memorized every construction zone in Nassau County.

When the Mazda's in motion, and I have to watch the road, we speculate on the secret lives of pedestrians and our fellow drivers. I'm not that creative, but Kendra's awesome at it. Maybe that's why she struggles to write for the school paper. The truth is never quite as interesting as something made up.

"See that guy in the Jeep Cherokee? He's got the spare tire stuffed with his ex-wives' heads."

I point to an innocent young woman pushing a newborn in a carriage. "And she's with the KGB."

"No, the *baby's* KGB," she corrects me. "The mother's a sophisticated robot. See? Her eyeballs are rotating camera lenses."

How am I supposed to keep up with that?

One time we pass a mild-mannered guy carrying a violin case, and she says, "Oh, *please*. There's no violin in there. That's a machine gun. I can spot a gangster a mile away."

God, I hope not.

I doubt she could ID my father or any of his associates. The fact is, we've all grown up with so many TV mobsters that, when you see the real thing, it's always a letdown. Dad could be the Pricewaterhouse representative who guards the ballots at the Academy Awards. Ray is a dead ringer for one of the priests at St. Bart's. Uncle Exit looks like exactly what he is, an aging hippie, complete with beads and tie-dye. He got arrested once for a homicide because the police found the impression of a peace sign in the strangulation marks on the victim's throat. He turned out to be innocent, but I can appreciate the cops' thinking process. The only difference between now and Uncle Exit's Woodstock days is that his shoulder-length hair is streaked with gray.

Uncle Puke is American Gothic without the pitchfork. Primo, this guy from his crew, is so into fishing that he walks around with a hatful of lures. And Uncle Carmine, who is a volunteer fireman in his other life, is just as likely to show up in a bright red fire-chief's car as in his Mercedes Kompressorwagen.

I pull over in front of the Y, and Kendra gets out.

"Need me to wait for you?" I ask. "I mean, this is a pretty tough neighborhood with all these wiseguys around." I indicate violin man, who, incidentally, is wearing a tux.

The truth is, dating someone who's busy is just as exhausting as being busy yourself. I may be just a moth to a flame, but every time the flame moves, I end up following it. And at least the flame has a purpose; I'm just flapping around.

Schoolwork gets done at midnight or not at all. But then, midnight has always been a busy time at the Luca house. Uncle Uncle has been underfoot lately, which usually means that a huge shipment of TVs or VCRs is about to fall off a truck at Kennedy Airport. It's almost like a plague of locusts when this happens. For a few days afterward, every drawer, every closet is packed with stolen goods. Swag, they call it. Around the time of the big Japan Airlines heist last year, I opened up my locker at school, and sixty brand-new Palm Pilots fell out. That's the last time I trusted Tommy with my combination.

Speak of the devil, Tommy's home too, peering over my shoulder and bugging me while I try to work on ILuvMyCat.

"How do you know all these cat owners?"

"I don't," I reply, keyboarding steadily. "But anybody with Internet access can get on my site."

"Anybody?"

"All you need is a computer and an Internet service provider. AOL. AT&T. My hookup is with the cable company. You just log on to my site and read what people have to say about their cats. You can post a message on my Cat Tales bulletin board and even e-mail a picture to go with it. Or if you're buying or selling a pet, you can place a free ad in Meow Marketplace."

I steel myself for his eruption of ridicule. Tommy isn't the most diplomatic guy in the world. But he's fascinated. "What's this ZIP-code thing? Why would you care where a bunch of strangers live?"

"That's for this other function," I explain. "Feline Friends Network. If you give me your ZIP code, I can match you with other cat lovers in your area who are interested in getting together to discuss their pets."

"Jeez, Vince," he says in genuine admiration. "I always knew you were smart, but I never thought you could do anything like this."

"It's not really as hard as it looks," I assure him. "You just have to work out the links. The program takes care of the rest."

He harrumphs. "In my world, a link is a sausage, and a program comes on TV."

I look at my brother, a guy who dropped out of eleventh grade, and who, to my knowledge, has never read a book from cover to cover. "Hey, Tommy, did you ever think of doing something with your life other than working with Dad and the uncles?"

He shrugs. "What else could a guy like me do?"

"Well, that's the whole thing," I persist. "You have no idea what you might be good at. You got on board with Dad before you could take a look at your options."

"There's nothing wrong with what Dad does!" he says hotly. "You drove a Porsche, and you'd be driving one today if you weren't such a boy scout!"

"You could go back to school—"

"Do you have any idea how much I hated school the first time around? Didn't you ever walk into a place, and you just know in your gut that it isn't for you? When you try, you fall flat on your face. And every rule they have seems like it was put there just to torture you."

I don't say anything, but Tommy has described exactly how I feel around the vending-machine business.

"What can I tell you, Vince? I'm not smart. But at least I'm smart enough to know it." He throws me a crooked grin. "You think I don't see how Dad brought in Ray to keep me out of trouble? He says Ray belongs to me, gives me points on his earnings. But you know what he really is? Screwup insurance. And the screwup is me."

"You could do worse than to listen to Ray," I say honestly. "He's a real friend. How he got mixed up in this crummy business is a mystery to me."

He's melancholy. "It's not just Ray. When Dad put me in charge of that thing with the cement-truck drivers, suddenly there's Uncle Fin watching my back. Or that Florida job, when Gus the Greek just *happened* to be on vacation down there. I look at those guys, and I *know* Dad tells them more about what's really going on than he tells me. He trusts strangers better than his own son. Dad's paranoid that the feds have an inside man in—" He catches himself; we're not in the basement. "Inside Brothers."

That's a jarring thought. We look at the FBI investigators as an amusing nuisance. You know, "Turn down the stereo, Tommy. Agent Numb-Nuts can't hear himself think." But an inside man posing as a wiseguy might be able to gather a lot of evidence. I mean, I don't think much of Dad's way of making a living, but sure don't want to see him go to jail. God, if they pin the Calabrese hit on Dad, that's a murder rap, guaranteed life sentence. And who knows what they could get Tommy on? And Ray and the uncles. They're all dirty. It would be like everybody I know suddenly disappearing.

"You're sure about that?" I ask nervously.

He shakes his head. "That's the whole point. I'll never know what Dad really thinks, because he doesn't believe I can keep my mouth shut. Even Mel knows more than me, and he's just some lawyer who happened to marry our sister. How can Dad be so sure Mel isn't the rat? He's not afraid of him."

"Because he's too busy being afraid of Mira," I quip, but add seriously, "I guess that's the whole thing about an inside man. It's always someone you don't suspect. Someone you trust."

"Well, then it can't be me," Tommy says sadly, "because Dad doesn't trust me as far as he can throw me. Not the way he trusts Mel. Or the way he would trust you."

"Dad knows I want nothing to do with The Life," I argue.

"I think he respects that more than anything," Tommy

informs me. "That you stand up to him. And he knows how smart you are. If he could see you doing this Bill Gates computer stuff, he'd blow up with pride."

Sometimes you talk to Tommy and it's almost like having a conversation with a human. A lot of brothers would carry plenty of resentment, feeling the way he does. But Tommy just tells it the way he sees it. He isn't a model citizen, but he has some good qualities just the same.

I stand up and sit him down in front of the keyboard. "The Internet isn't rocket science," I say kindly. "Here, let me show you. . . ."

[NINE]

GRIM NEWS ON THE **A**LEX FRONT. Fiona, this girl in our New Media class, e-mails him at MisterFerrariDriver to congratulate him on his Web site. And to Alex, this equals a declaration of undying lust. But when he asks her out, she says no.

"She's evil," he laments after school the day it happens. "She led me on just so she could slap me down."

"She didn't lead you on," I try to explain. "She heard you talking about your site in class, and she checked it out. That's it."

"She says she has a boyfriend in Canada," he moans. "What a crock. Whenever chicks make up a boyfriend, he's always Canadian. Nobody ever puts the fake boyfriend in Uzbekistan."

"Maybe she's telling the truth," Kendra says soothingly.

"She's the devil," Alex growls.

Believe it or not, this is more or less all my fault. In the old days, Alex would have told me about the e-mail from Fiona, and I would have had a chance to prepare him for the possibility that this was just a friendly message from a classmate. But I was with Kendra last night, incommunicado, and very happily so. I can just picture Alex, sitting at his computer, reading the e-mail for the fiftieth time, building the whole thing up in his mind until he's convinced himself that the girl is crazy about him. So when he gets rejected, he's devastated.

I know Alex, so I realize that now's the time to stop arguing and start agreeing. Yes, he's been badly wronged; Fiona is Public Enemy Number One, and it's a travesty that there isn't some kind of international tribunal empowered to handle this kind of injustice.

Unfortunately, Kendra doesn't have the benefit of my experience. She thinks Alex can be reasoned with.

"Maybe it just wasn't meant to be," she offers gently.

"Meant to be?" Alex wails. "What are you, Oprah?"

"Alex—" I begin warningly.

"That didn't come out right," she admits. "What I'm trying to say is that, even if she went out with you, it still doesn't guarantee that it'd lead anywhere. Some people are just wrong for each other."

His expression scares me because I know what's coming. If I had a gag, believe me, I'd use it.

"That's a good point, Kendra," he says, a little too conversationally. "I know a couple who *really* don't belong together. I mean, this is practically like a cobra dating a mongoose. Can you imagine a—"

I grab Kendra by the arm. "Let's go. You'll be late for work." As I hustle her out the door, Alex's unspoken words resonate in my head: *Can you imagine a Mob prince going out with an FBI agent's daughter?*

I cast him a look designed to freeze lava, focusing all my being into a single message: *Don't go there.*

I'm surprised by the fear on his face. It's possible that I've just conjured up the Luca Stare. Tommy can do it, and Dad's an expert. But this is the first time I've ever come up with it on my own. I'm not proud of it, but Alex has crossed the line here. He has to know that it's time to scramble back to his own side.

Kendra is bewildered. "Vince, what just happened there?"

"Alex's cousin is getting divorced," I lie smoothly. "He's pretty upset about it, but I wasn't going to let him take it out on you."

We head for the parking lot. I can see right away that there's someone sitting on my car. But it isn't until we're almost there that I realize who it is. I hardly recognize him without the black eye, split lip, and caked-on blood.

"Jimmy Rat!"

Jimmy slides down off the hood. "I recognized your vehicle." No small feat for a guy who only saw the inside of the trunk. "How's it going, Vince?"

It's an awkward moment. I should introduce Kendra, but this is a guy who sometimes talks to my dad. So I just ask, "What are you doing at my school?"

"Excuse us, Miss," he says to her and pulls me aside. "I got something for your father." From the pocket of his blazer, he pulls out a fat money-size envelope. "Give him this, will you?"

I make no move to take it. "Why don't you give it to him

yourself? Or shouldn't there be someone to collect this? Uncle Shank, or one of his guys?"

He shuffles and wriggles at the same time, and his nose twitches. I can see where he gets his nickname, and not just from being James Ratelli. "The envelope is a little lighter than it's supposed to be. And your uncle Shank's kind of touchy about stuff like that. Your father, too, and definitely your brother. But you, Vince—you're a reasonable person. I can see that from our past dealings."

"What past dealings?" I catch a questioning look from Kendra, so I drop my voice. "We don't have any past dealings! You were locked in the trunk of my car!"

"And you were very reasonable about it," he repeats. "You'll have no problem explaining to your old man that I need a few more days to come up with the rest of the money. Tell him how sincere I am."

"No!" I explode. "I have nothing to do with that business! Listen, Jimmy, I'm sorry you're in trouble, but you'll just have to find another way out."

He grabs me by the front of my jacket. "Have a heart, Vince!" he sobs. "Shank's got a thing about cutting off fingers! If they break your nose, you still got a nose! But fingers don't grow back!"

Right there in the parking lot I have a murky flashback. I must have been eight or nine. Alex and I ride up the driveway on our bikes. A handful of uncles are in the side yard, Tommy with them. It was right after he quit school to work with Dad. I remember the excited laughing chatter that always came in the aftermath of a "job," although back then I don't know what "jobs" are all about. Uncle Shank—and I remember this clearly—is standing at the outdoor water tap, a big grin on his face. He's rinsing off the sharp blades of a pair of pruning shears.

For a second, I feel like I'm going to pass out. I think I might fall over if Jimmy doesn't still have a death grip on my jacket.

I snatch the envelope out of his hand. "I—I'll see what I can do."

Jimmy's all over me, blubbering and kissing my hand. I'm trying to pull away, babbling, "This might not work! I don't know if they'll listen to me!" I hate my dad right now. The fact that I might wield such power over a person's fate makes me want to cry. But I hold back because part of me is wondering what in God's green earth I'm going to tell Kendra about all this.

I get her into the car and peel out of there with a squeal of tires. I must be pretty shaken up because she comments, "What happened with that guy, Vince? You look like you've just seen a ghost."

And I have. The image of those pruning shears gleaming wet in the sunlight doesn't go away.

Bellmore Preschool is located in an old elementary school a few towns to the east of us. The day care is on the ground floor, with a senior center on the second level. This, Kendra explains, is ironic because it's difficult for the seniors to negotiate the stairs, but the kids always seem to have enough energy to sprint up the side of Mount Everest.

She works in the toddler room—two-year-olds. They seem to love her because they all run over to give her a hug. Then they give me a hug, and I realize that two-year-olds don't know much.

I remember the head lice and switch to shaking hands. The kids stare at me like I'm nuts.

Five minutes in that place and I understand why Kendra is so exhausted after work. We play games; we sing songs; we march; we dance.

"When's nap time?" I ask hopefully.

Bad news. We just missed it.

Thumper, the class rabbit, escapes his cage, and all hell breaks loose. In the melee, a little girl runs up and gives me a small piece of paper. I gawk. It's a hundred-dollar bill.

"What the—?"

A little boy flashes by, and he's got a fistful of money.

I have an irrational thought: What kind of parents send their two-year-olds to day care with bankrolls in their pockets?

Then I see it. The chair where I hung my jacket is lying over on its side, and Jimmy Rat's envelope is half out of my pocket. Little kids are climbing all over each other to get their share of the money.

I run around like a wild man, snatching bills out of very small hands. Kids being kids, they fly into temper tantrums. I don't care. Jimmy Rat entrusted me with this money, and I don't even know how much is supposed to be there, but the payment is light and getting lighter. Even the rabbit is nibbling on a fifty. Who knows how much the hamster has squirreled away?

Now I'm at the center of a Hallelujah chorus of tears and rage. Kendra and her coworkers are furious.

"Vince, what's going—?" She goggles at the small fortune wadded in my hands. "Where did you get all that money?"

"From the kids!" I shout back without thinking.

"What?"

Now I've done it. I've got no choice but to explain that Jimmy gave me the money for Dad.

She's amazed. "What kind of business is your father in?"

"He's in investments," I reply, thinking on my feet.

"Like Wall Street?"

"Exactly. Only he doesn't go into the city. He works out here on the Island."

"Wall Street doesn't trade envelopes full of hundred-dollar bills," she says suspiciously. "All that's done electronically."

Heart sinking, I notice she's wearing her reporter's face. All the slack she cut me in the parking lot because I was upset is gone. I've got to find a way to come clean without actually coming clean. A sick feeling takes hold in the pit of my stomach as it sinks in that my next tap dance will determine whether or not I've still got a girlfriend five minutes from now.

"That guy Jimmy—obviously you can tell that he isn't exactly the prince of England. A real bank would take one look at him and say, forget it. That's where my father comes in. His company invests in people like Jimmy, and because it's outside the normal banking system, some of the payments are made in cash."

"You mean like a social service?" she asks. "Banking for the underprivileged?"

"Right." Isn't Kendra fantastic? Anthony Luca has teams of lawyers working for him, and I'll bet none of them have ever hit on such a positive way to describe loan-sharking.

"Hey," she says suddenly. "Do you think your dad would let me interview him for the *Journal*? I'll bet most of the kids haven't even heard of his job."

"My father never talks about business," I reply quickly. "It's the number one rule at our house."

She nods wisely. "My dad is exactly the same way. He's a clam about work. When I was younger some evidence got destroyed at home, and now he won't even tell Mom what cases he's working on."

Yeah, right. Honest Abe Luca and Agent Bite-Me of the FBI. Sometimes I have trouble telling them apart.

Dad takes Jimmy Rat's envelope, but he doesn't look at it. His eyes stay focused on me. "How come you're doing Uncle Shank's job for him?"

We're in the basement workshop, sitting uncomfortably on lopsided furniture. Ray and Tommy are there too. I'm trying not to stare at an enormous pine hutch, the latest project. It stands about ten feet away, with a claw hammer embedded in the cracked side, eloquent testament to Dad's temper.

"I'm not," I argue. "It's just that Jimmy came to me to ask you for more time."

"He's using you, Vince!" Tommy explodes. "Do I have to put that bag of guts back in the car again?"

"No!" I say quickly. "He wanted to talk to me because Uncle Shank makes him nervous."

"That's the whole point of having a guy like Shank," Ray explains. "To keep the Jimmy Rats of this world nice and nervous."

"You should have seen him, Dad," I plead. "He's terrified! He thinks Uncle Shank is going to cut off his fingers."

Dad leans back and very nearly overturns his ill-balanced chair. "You want no part of this business, Vince. Fair enough. So where do you get off telling me how to run it?"

I'm on the verge of preaching when I catch a warning glance from Ray and back right off. It's nothing Anthony Luca hasn't heard a million times from me, the FBI, the media, and an outraged populace. He was in The Life before I was born, and I'm not going to come up with any words tonight that will change his mind about it. Besides, it sure won't help Jimmy Rat if I make my father mad.

So I say, "It's just six hundred bucks. What's that much money to you?"

"It's never just six hundred from Jimmy Rat," Ray puts in. "It's a lot of six hundreds from a lot of Jimmy Rats. A guy like that—dumb, likeable, goofy. I don't want to see him get hurt, but I don't want to see *us* get hurt when the word spreads we don't stick up for ourselves."

I'm taking hits from Ray and Tommy, but I keep plugging away at Dad. "Aw, he's such a loser, and you're so powerful. Leave him alone, okay? I'm sure that if you give him a chance to get back on track, you'll get your money."

"You don't know what you're talking about!" Tommy

roars. "You're letting this two-bit beer hustler snow you!"

But Dad quiets him with a single look. Then he turns his gaze on me. "Seventeen years I've been waiting, Vince, to see what brings out the fire in you. And this is it? Jimmy Rat? I'll bet he gave you the whole sob story about his wife and kids. Would it surprise you to know the guy's a lifelong bachelor?"

I don't back down. "Just give him a break, Dad. Please."

My father stands up. "He gets one week. And it's on *you* for every cent he comes up short."

Tommy's horrified. "Dad! If we go soft on a little creep like that, no one'll respect us out on the street!"

"We're not going soft," Dad insists. "Jimmy's got Vince vouching for him now. You got a beef with Jimmy, you talk to Vince."

I'm not so sure I like the sound of that. But I don't want to push it, so I say, "Thanks, Dad. You won't regret this."

Ray steps in. "If word gets around that the way to miss a vig is to talk to Vince, that high school is going to need a bigger parking lot."

"That's Vince's problem," my father replies. To me he says, "I hope you know what you're getting into."

I hope so too.

[TEN]

I CALL JIMMY RAT AT THE ONLY number I have for him, the phone behind the bar at his place of business, a club called Return to Sender. I wonder if he gets any mail with a name like that. Certainly no one's there early enough to straighten out misunderstandings with the letter carrier—I try him all day without results. By the time I get through, I'm on the road to pick up Kendra.

I know this sounds impossible, but when he finally comes on the line, I can actually *hear* the smoke. He cries when I give him the good news, and I get warm all over. I know I've done something special, not just for Jimmy, but for Dad and Tommy too. I've saved them from committing one more immoral act. While that may seem like a drop in the bucket, it feels very big to me.

"So you're off the hook till next Friday," I finish. "Let's meet on Thursday afternoon so you can give me the money."

"Yeah, sure," he agrees. "I'll find you."

A tiny alarm bell goes off in the back of my mind. "I think we should set a specific time—"

Somehow the connection gets broken, and I can't dial in again. Probably a problem on his end, since my cell phone is brand-new.

I never pick Kendra up at home unless I know her folks aren't there. We always meet somewhere. Today we hook up outside the Barnes and Noble where I supposedly work—one of my ersatz jobs. I may not have a future in the vending-machine business, but I sure seem to have the deceit part down pat. It's nice to know that dating brings out the best in me.

"How was work?" she asks, sliding in beside me.

"Oh, same old, same old." Our fingers intertwine over the gearshift console.

"What are we doing tonight?"

"It's a surprise," I tell her.

She goes nuts trying to guess what it is, but I don't spill the beans. Eventually, we're tooling up Sunrise Highway with her clamped on to me, half on the driver's seat, begging.

"See that guy?" I point to a frail elderly man laboriously extricating himself from a parked Volkswagen Beetle. "Santa Claus on Slim-Fast."

She isn't taking the bait. "Come on. Just tell me."

I'm enjoying myself so much pulling her chain that I actually pass by the place before circling back into the parking lot.

Rio Grande is a Mexican restaurant, but the thing is there's a karaoke bar too, so Kendra can take her act on the road in front of a real audience.

She turns pale. "I can't do it."

"Sure you can," I coax. "You're awesome!"

"No."

Well, we have to eat anyway—that's the logic I use to get her in the door. Maybe an enchilada will change her mind.

The food is good. Everything is so fiery hot that we're downing pitchers of Coke like water after a marathon. By eight o'clock, when the singing starts, we're both wired from sugar and caffeine. Our table is in a ring of booths around the central bar part, so we're right in the middle of the action.

The first few "performers" flat-out stink. Rio Grande resounds with laughter and catcalls, but the singers shriek and mumble on, even as they are pelted with cherries and tortilla chips. I'm horrified at the raw cruelty, but it slowly sinks in that this is the whole gig here. These people know how terrible they are, and the louder the audience boos, the more they play to it.

Kendra's mesmerized as if we're watching the parting of the Red Sea, and not some three-hundred-pound guy singing "I'm Too Sexy. . . ." Actually, he's the only one this crowd seems to like. He gets a standing ovation, especially when he rips open the shirt he's too sexy for. It brings the house down.

I try to put my arm around Kendra's shoulders, but she's totally rigid. I start to consider that this might be a bad idea. A local college girl is singing Motown—and she's actually pretty decent—when I softly suggest, "Maybe we should get out of here."

Kendra points to the stage. "Is she really that good?"

"I never said she was—" Then I realize the true meaning of the question. "Kendra, you blow her away."

She takes a deep breath, combs her blond hair with her fingers, and straightens her blouse. "If I stink, I hate your guts for bringing me here."

I get a warm glow. If the reverse holds true, she's going to love me.

When Hannibal pointed his elephants at the Alps and yelled *giddyup*, he had the same look in his eyes as Kendra, marching over to that microphone.

She's a showstopper. Well, not exactly, but nobody throws any fruit at her, and that's a big deal with this crowd. She starts off nervous, but really loosens up, belting out everything from "What a Girl Wants" to "Stairway to Heaven." By her third or fourth song, she's picking up a core of fans. Remember, this place is also a bar. We're not drinking, but everybody else is, and the crowd's appreciation of the music seems to rise with their intoxication level.

"You're a smash!" I crow.

She grabs my arm. "Get up here!"

"But I can't—"

"I need a backup singer!"

Well, maybe Kendra doesn't stink, but I *do*. I take a few direct hits from maraschino cherries, but nothing touches her. Highly selective abusers, this crowd.

We're back at the table when in walks a tall cadaverous man in black slacks and turtleneck. I almost inhale my straw when I recognize the guy. It's a good thing there's music on because I think I scream. It's Uncle Pampers.

The thought of Uncle Pampers in a karaoke bar kind of makes me want to laugh and be sick at the same time. He holds a special place in Dad's organization. He doesn't hang out with the other uncles. I'm pretty sure they're afraid of him. Quite frankly, I think Dad might be too. That's where the nickname comes from. If you open your door and see Uncle Pampers standing there, you—ahem—you get the picture. "I hope he's got his Pampers on," the uncles used to joke whenever he got sent to pay a visit to somebody.

At least, that's Tommy's version. I only talked to Dad about Uncle Pampers once, and he got pretty uncomfortable about it, as if we were discussing the birds and the bees. The official job description is "problem solver." As in: "You got a problem, you call up your Uncle Pampers, and he makes it go away." I've also heard it as "troubleshooter," with an ominous emphasis on *shoot*, although Tommy assures me that Uncle Pampers prefers to work more quietly. Mario Calabrese, for example, was strangled with the cord from his own Walkman while jogging. Naturally, the case remains unsolved. But if it's true that Dad gave the order, the job was almost certainly carried out by Uncle Pampers.

Nobody ever said explicitly that the "problems" he solves are actual people. I kind of figured it out from the way the other uncles, their wives, and even Dad stay away from him. At family gatherings he plays with the little kids. I used to assume he loves children, but now I realize that they're the only ones who can look at him without thinking about what he does to make a buck.

And here he is at Rio Grande. I shrink a little lower in my seat. The last thing I need is a friendly how's-it-going chat with a professional killer. That's a definite dating no-no—right up there with having an unconscious guy in your trunk. Especially when the date is with Kendra, whose father probably has a file on Uncle Pampers that's even thicker than the one on Dad.

He takes a sip of his drink and steps up to the microphone. With each passing second, this night is turning into a comic opera of the absurd. Uncle Pampers singing? This I've got to hear!

Twangy guitar swells, and the Grim Reaper of the vending-machine business launches into a whiny, nasal rendition of an old country song called "The Lowdown Blues."

A cocktail umbrella bounces off his nose, and I hold my breath, waiting for Uncle Pampers to perform the first-ever karaoke bar splenectomy. But he keeps wailing away. And because the music is so grating, it takes everybody a minute to realize how *fantastic* he is. He's not just singing—he's moaning, howling, lamenting, and yodeling. *Yodeling!* If somebody told me that either the moon was going to fall out of the sky, or Uncle Pampers would yodel, I'd stack all my chips on the moon. But here he is, putting on a performance worthy of Hank Williams himself. And not Junior. I'm talking about Hank Williams *Senior*!

When he finishes, Rio Grande rocks with thunderous applause. Uncle Pampers has pulled off the karaoke feat of the century. I'll bet not a single soul in the building actually likes that kind of music, yet he won them over. I mean, he usually wins people over. But this time he didn't have to threaten to kill them. Oblivious to the adulation, he returns to the bar to sip quietly at his drink.

Kendra's face is pink with excitement. "That was *awesome!*" she raves. "Let's go congratulate him!"

Uh-oh. "He seems like a pretty private person," I put in quickly. "Maybe we should leave him alone."

It takes a while for the place to get back to normal. Nobody wants to be the act to follow Uncle Pampers. Eventually some poor sap decides to brave the abuse, and things get rolling again. Kendra goes up a few more times, but I demur from my backup singing job—at least until Uncle Pampers leaves. He gives an encore performance of yodelmania before he takes off, singing a pathetic song about a broken-down pickup truck and a three-legged dog.

I breathe a sigh of relief once he's gone.

It's almost eleven when I finally signal our waitress. She shoots me a questioning look.

"We're ready for our check."

She seems confused. "It's already been taken care of."

I'm amazed. "By who?"

"The tall man who sings Hank Williams. Good tipper, too."

All the way out, Kendra is on my case. "Why didn't you tell me you know him?"

"Because I don't," I defend myself. "He's just a guy who sometimes does—odd jobs for my father. I wasn't even sure it was him at first."

She doesn't say anything, but I catch a glimpse of her

reporter's face as we head out to the parking lot. Either that or it's the expression of someone who can spot a gangster a mile away after she's just heard one yodeling.

Everything's okay back in the Mazda, though. We fold readily into an embrace that's become both exciting and familiar. "I had a great time, Vince," she murmurs in my ear. "Thanks for making me have the guts to do it."

"You were the hit of the show," I assure her. Strictly speaking, she was only runner up, but I'm definitely not in the mood to bring up Uncle Pampers again.

"Hey, what are you doing next Friday?" she asks suddenly.

"This," I reply, kissing her.

"Seriously," she laughs, pushing me away. "How about dinner at my house?"

They say when you're in a car accident, there's a split second where you know what's going to happen, but you can't do anything about it. That's me. Agent Bite-Me's dinner table is hurtling toward me at sixty miles an hour, and my foot can't find the brake pedal.

She senses something is wrong. "What?"

"Nothing. It's just that—you told your parents about me?"

"Of course. Well, my mom, anyway. My father's been working a lot. I haven't really seen him all that much. But they're not stupid, Vince. They can tell I've been dating somebody."

"Well, uh"—I'm grasping at straws—"do we really have to bring parents into it already? I mean we've only been going out for three weeks."

She's bewildered. "It's not like we're meeting at the caterers to pick out hors d'oeuvres for our wedding! It's just dinner. My girlfriends come over all the time. What's so different about this?"

For starters, your dad isn't bugging any of their houses. "What we've got, Kendra—it's going so great. I guess it's just that I don't want to mess with it. And bringing parents in might change things."

She looks troubled. "What are you saying? You'll never meet my parents, and I'll never meet yours?"

"Of course not," I protest, but in reality, I can't see how it could work any other way. "Let's keep it just our thing a while longer. Then our relationship will be rock solid, and we'll be able to handle the pressures."

Our thing. What an unfortunate choice of words. In Italian, "our thing" translates as *cosa nostra*.

She's more than merely silent. She's silent with extreme prejudice. In her eyes, I've just crossed a line.

"What?" I ask gently.

She shakes her head. "I don't know. It's like there's something you're not telling me. Like you have a secret life."

I try to make a joke out of it. "Everybody has a secret life. At least everybody we pass in the car. Remember that nun who worked for the Mossad. . . ."

My voice trails off. She's not letting me get away with it. She's really mad.

"Something's not right. I don't know if it's you or me, but something's messed up, here."

"It's just temporary," I plead. "When we've been going out a little bit longer, I promise this'll be no big deal."

She eyes me suspiciously. "But it'll happen eventually, right? Dinner with my folks?"

"Oh, sure. Eventually."

The next ice age is coming eventually, too.

[ELEVEN]

"**HEY, VINCE, HOW COME YOU NEVER** told me you got a girl-friend?"

I'm trying to check up on ILuvMyCat, but Tommy's hogging my computer. Ever since my mini lesson, he's been hooked. Actually, I'm more impressed than annoyed. I never would have pegged my brother as the Web-surfer type.

"She's not my girlfriend," I say quickly. "We've only been dating a few weeks. Who told you? Did you bludgeon it out of Alex?"

"Nah," he chuckles, "Uncle Pampers saw you and her at some burrito joint."

"Uncle Pampers came here last night?" It's only Sunday morning.

He nods. "Business thing."

Unbelievable. The guy went straight from yodeling to doing business. *Business!*

Tommy notices the look of distaste on my face. "Take it

easy, Elliot Ness. We just needed him to go with No-Nose to make a point with somebody. Friend of your buddy Jimmy Rat."

My brother hasn't shut up for two seconds about the Jimmy Rat thing. There he's found a surprise ally in Ray. But while Tommy raves about how Dad's gone crazy, Ray just thinks it's bad business. I'm not so sure. Anthony Luca may be a lot of things, but he's not stupid.

If there's an undercover agent in the organization somewhere, maybe Dad thinks that throwing me into the mix might confuse him. After all, the vending-machine business is as organized as a Roman legion, complete with captains and soldiers and a chain of command. Turning loose a squeaky-clean seventeen-year-old civilian on an errand of mercy could mislead the investigation. Especially me, because the uncles never know quite what to make of me.

On the one hand, I'm an outsider, and that's by Dad's orders. On the other, I'm the boss's son, which is as inside as you can get. Either way, they have to deal with me, if for no other reason than the fact that our house is like vending-machine headquarters, and Mom's dinner table is the commissary. For good or ill, we're doomed to tread the same real estate. I can't even count the number of times I've padded barefoot down to the kitchen for breakfast only to find myself sharing the coffeepot with some uncle or soldier who hasn't been to bed yet. And when my bleary eyes finally focus, I notice he's holding an ice pack over his head where he's obviously been hit by a pipe or a baseball bat. But we can't talk about that because I'm "out." So we discuss the weather or the Knicks game while we drink coffee, and he bleeds, and I ask myself, Is this really happening, or is it part of some weird dream directed by Fellini? God only knows what these guys think of me.

If there is an inside man, he's already confused by my role. Sending me to collect from a deadbeat could be the perfect smokescreen.

More likely, though, Dad's just letting me fool around. He thinks I'm unmotivated, so he wants to see what happens when I put my mind to something. It's like when a farmer gives his kid a baby sheep or pig to take care of. Jimmy Rat is my barnyard pet, which seems totally appropriate as far as the guy's personal grooming is concerned. I'm not sure exactly how it works on the farm, but I have a sneaking suspicion that those animals end up in the slaughterhouse along with all the others. Then the kids learn the lesson that the world can be a cold and ruthless place.

I hope that's not the plan for Jimmy Rat and me.

Tommy stands up, and I take my place at the keyboard. "Don't get me wrong, Vince. I'm thrilled that you're finally getting some. When you blew off Cece, I thought you were—"

"Listen," I interrupt, "I've got a lot of work to do." Did Wally ever have this conversation with the Beaver?

The Web sites for New Media are all up and running, and some of them are starting to generate a handful of hits. Mr. Mullinicks assures us that most of the early action is from proud parents, aunts, and uncles. That explains why ILuvMyCat is lagging behind some of the others—the only computers in the possession of my relatives are being sold off the back of a truck.

Much to Alex's dismay, Fiona, who he now calls The Hated One, boasts the class's top site, CyberPharaoh. She's an ancient Egypt buff, which is kind of cool, I think. In Alex's eyes, she'll never be forgiven for not being an Alex Tarkanian buff.

"What a joke!" he snorts. "Do you have any idea how many Egyptology sites are out there?"

"Well, there must also be a whole lot of closet Egyptologists," I reply, "because she got over a hundred hits in the first week."

"I hope a pyramid rolls over on her," he mutters. "Egyptology. Stick this in your sphinx." (Obscene gesture.)

MisterFerrariDriver comes in a surprise second with sixty hits. I'm positive that not a single one of those originates from a person who actually drives a Ferrari. Judging by the writing on the bulletin board postings, I'd say the vehicle of choice among Alex's constituency is a tricycle.

But I don't have much to say about it, because thus far I've received a grand total of one hit. It's from an eighty-five-year-old lady in Maryland. She's not even technically a real cat owner, because her cat died over the summer. But that doesn't stop her from telling Fluffy's entire life story on Cat Tales. I'm not exactly the star of the class.

Until that Sunday. I log on to the Internet and call up ILuvMyCat. I stare at the counter. Forty-seven.

Forty-six hits in one night!

Excitedly, I browse through my features. Cat Tales still

stands at one with the message from the octogenarian. Nothing in Feline Friends Network. All the new action is in Meow Marketplace, where there are *twenty-three* new ads! Yeah, there are a lot of pet owners out there, but the ones on my site don't seem to be a very loyal group. They're either trying to get rid of their cats or looking for new ones.

I pull up the first ad:

> **I'm selling my third-favorite cat, Lady Anne. She's a real winner, pure gold. $200—SG.**

I frown. I'm not expecting Shakespeare here, but who's going to buy an animal based on that? And why say she's only your third favorite? That sounds kind of cruel to me. It certainly wouldn't make me feel very good to find out I'm Mom's third favorite kid.

I call up another:

> **Who wants to buy a real show cat for only 300 bucks? Dakota Glory is a little inky, but he can high-five you—MT.**

Inky? Does that mean a black cat? I keep going:

> **If you're looking for a prime minister of a cat, you've come to the right place. Dynamico caught three mice last week. Only $100—AS.**

A "prime minister" of a cat? I page down. They're all like that. And the *names*! What kind of an idiot names his cat Motherlode or Under the Rainbow? Sure, Mr. Mullinicks warned us that we'd probably run into a few weirdos online. But on ILuvMyCat *everybody*'s a weirdo!

I'm selling exactly two of my cats, Kensington and Scattered Showers. You've never seen such a couple of movie stars. They're number one! $200 for the pair—CC.

I don't want to be nitpicky, especially with something that's so bizarre to start with. But how can *two* cats be number one?

Alex thinks I'm making a mountain out of a molehill. "Compared to the dweebs pretending to own Ferraris out there, your cat owners are pretty normal," he assures me in class on Monday. "You should spend a few hours on MisterFerrariDriver. I've never seen such a bunch of nerds in my life. You can picture their mothers ironing the pocket protectors of their short-sleeved shirts. I'll bet most of them are nine."

"At least you can explain yours," I say. "My postings are surreal. You couldn't make them up if you tried."

He looks me squarely in the eye. "Maybe *Kendra* can help you figure it out."

That's Alex's new M.O. He deflects everything back to Kendra. Last week I remembered I left my old jockstrap from football in the Jaguars locker room. When I recruited Alex to check the lost-and-found box at the next practice, he sneered, "Why don't you ask *Kendra* to get it for you?"

Very subtle, my friend Alex.

I play dumb. "Kendra doesn't even own a cat." But I can't hide anything from Alex; he's been my confidant since grade school. "Besides, she's kind of miffed at me. She invited me to have dinner with her folks, and obviously that can't happen, so she says I'm avoiding her family."

"You *are* avoiding her family," he points out.

"You got that right."

Just the notion that there might be some trouble in paradise animates Alex. "You know, Vince, even if you can keep on dodging her parents, you're not out of the woods. I mean, how long before she happens to mention that she's dating a guy named Luca?"

I say nothing. It's not that I don't see his point. Sure, it would make the most sense to break up right now, before Kendra ever has a clue who my father is. But I can't do it. My family has cost me so much already—to the point where I can't even go on a date, or play on a stupid high-school football team. They won't cost me this.

Besides, I'm an addict. I'm hooked.

As the week goes on, the cat owners of America continue to visit ILuvMyCat, not to do anything else on the site, but just to place ads on Meow Marketplace. Not one of these listings gets a single response, but the ads keep coming:

Want me to show you a real gem of a cat with four on the floor? Robert E. Lee's the name, and he can be yours for 250 bucks—SK.

Again, nitpicky, but don't all cats technically have four on the floor?

If you're going to a toga party, Equilibrium is the perfect cat to take there. He's a real eight ball with a winning smile. Only $350 —TC.

By Wednesday, I'm in third place in the class, trailing only CyberPharaoh and MisterFerrariDriver. And the strange postings on my site have come to the attention of my fellow students. .

"Hey, Vince," calls Martin Antia. "I've got a cat to sell, too. He's no prime minister, but maybe he can lick himself at the toga party just for laughs."

"Shut up," I groan.

"Yeah, what's going on?" puts in Yuri, this Russian kid with a last name I won't attempt to reproduce. "You've got dozens of ads, but the rest of your site is empty."

"If you've got some cousin dreaming it all up," adds Fiona, "tell him he's got a real future in Hollywood."

It doesn't take much to get Alex mobilized on my behalf when Fiona's the enemy. "ILuvMyCat is a hundred-percent legit!" he snaps. "It's going to smoke your crummy site, that's for sure."

"Take it easy," I say soothingly. "If I had someone inventing that stuff, don't you think I'd get him to make it a little more believable? And to spread it around the site? The fact is I'm as mystified as you guys."

I even raise the subject with Mr. Mullinicks. Not that I'm a crybaby, but the Internet can be a wild and woolly place, so it's probably a good idea for an expert to take a look at ILuvMyCat.

He calls up my site on his desktop and browses through the ads, now more than a hundred. Finally, he says, "I don't know much about cat ownership."

"Me neither," I confess. "But I'm pretty sure this isn't it. Could it be some kind of Internet pattern, you know, something you've seen before?"

"Oh, I've seen it before," he assures me.

"Really?"

He nods. "It's called 'your problem.'"

"But—"

"It's definitely *your* problem, because if it was somebody else's, it wouldn't be on *your* Web site."

"But I was kind of hoping—"

He cuts me off. "Vince, let me give you a little friendly advice. You're getting hits—that's all that matters. What do you care if they don't make any sense? The e-business economy isn't about sense; it's about traffic. Don't argue with success. A week ago your site was a wasteland."

I make it sound as if the whole school is obsessed with ILuvMyCat. The truth is, outside of New Media, no one else has a clue. It's a typical October. The weather cools down.

Clothing gets less revealing, much to Alex's dismay. I initiate the annual discarding of notices home advising my parents about Open House. Freshman year, Mom volunteered for the refreshments committee and baked so many cookies that Dad had to arrange for a union truck to come from New Jersey to deliver them. But some wires got crossed on a job Uncle Puke and his crew had going in Staten Island. So when the tractor-trailer pulled up to the gym, it was full of hot digital watches from Taiwan. Actually, it worked out okay because the watches were a hit at school, and when the cops arrested Uncle Puke and searched his truck, they found nothing but oatmeal-raisin cookies.

Mom tried to get her refreshments back, but the truck was impounded in an FBI warehouse. "In this heat," she lamented, "those cookies are totally out of commission by now. Such a shame to waste good food."

She wasn't going to get away with it this time! I was positive she knew more than she let on.

"But, Mom," I persisted. "What about the watches? Where did they come from?"

"Switzerland," she replied without missing a beat. Very cool under fire. I think it rubs off on her from Dad.

Classes seem longer. Homework gets harder, or at least there's more of it. The Jaguars hold pep rallies nobody goes to. Colorful signs begin to decorate the blah cinderblock walls, promoting the popular kids for homecoming king and queen.

I almost drop dead. Outside the cafeteria, in the midst of a forest of posters about quarterbacks and cheerleaders, is a computer-generated message printed in huge letters on continuous paper:

VOTE VINCE L. & KENDRA B. FOR K & Q

I just stand there like an idiot, reading it over and over, my head bobbing back and forth, like a spectator at a tennis match. I swear that, as I try to make sense of this new development, the thought actually crosses my mind that they might be talking about two other kids with our names.

Then, from behind: "Who are Vince L. and Kendra B.?"

I wheel to face the sophomore girl. "Nobody!" I exclaim, pulling the poster off the wall.

Talk about a worst-case scenario. Homecoming is a big deal at our school. The king and queen are practically local celebrities. They get interviewed in the paper, and their smiling mugs are displayed in every bagel shop and dry cleaner in town. Keeping Kendra and me secret—forget about it. And not just from Agent Bite-Me. From Tommy and Dad, too.

I mean, Kendra and I have no chance of winning, but still! This is like juggling nitro. Who would do such a thing?

I corner Kendra in front of her locker at the next class change. "Look at this!" I spit, dropping our sign at her feet.

She bends down and unfurls the crumpled computer paper. Her face lights up.

I stare at her in horror. "You did this!"

"No, I didn't!"

But there's no stopping Sherlock Holmes when he's

cracking a case. "You're mad because I won't have dinner with your parents, so you want to get us voted homecoming king and queen because then we'll have to go public."

"You're on drugs," she accuses me. "I've never seen this poster before now, but that's not even the weird part. The real killer is that 'going public' is something we have to decide to do, like we're secret agents blowing our cover. We're just dating, Vince. Millions of kids do it. What's the big whoop?"

"It's too soon," I say stubbornly.

"You're ashamed of me!"

"No—" I start to protest.

"Of our relationship, then."

"That's not it."

She's steamed. "Well, then you're just plain lazy. You don't want to admit you've got a girlfriend because I'm not worth a little explaining."

That stings, and it isn't just because Kendra's so mad at me. Lazy—it's dangerously close to Dad's motivation speech. Pick a college—ahem, *university*—pick a career, get off your butt and *do* something. I remember Ray's words: "Enjoy it. It's never going to be this new again." Oh, sure. First girlfriend. First relationship. First knock-down dragout fight.

Yeah, I know couples argue all the time. But that's never happened with Kendra and me. I want to stop it—just say we're more important and find some secluded corner and—

No. Part of me is too upset, and the upset part is on

autopilot. I crumple up the sign and slamdunk it in a trash can. "I better not find out this was you."

"Yeah, I trust you too," she snaps back at me, and we storm off in different directions.

Later, in her basement, we make up, and everything feels so perfect. But even an addict has lucid moments, and here's mine: There are two different relationships—the short-term us and the long-term us. When the time horizon is, let's say, three hours or less, we're unstoppable. But expand that from hours to months and it all starts to fray. Kendra doesn't know where we're going, and, worse, I know exactly where we're going.

The long-term us has always been doomed.

Maybe I'm being overly fatalistic because, while all this is happening, the clock is ticking on Jimmy Rat. I place dozens of calls each day to Return to Sender, but nobody answers except late at night. And then I only reach a lady bartender with a gravelly voice who refuses to take a message. I see that Jimmy brings out in his employees the same kind of loyalty and respect that he gets from Tommy and Dad.

"Listen, I only work here," she assures me again and again. "You got something to say to Jimmy, you tell him yourself."

It's so hard to find good help these days.

I finally get through on Friday afternoon.

"Hey, Vince. What's up?"

"What's up?" I echo. "The time's up, that's what's up! Today's the day you have to pay that money to my dad!"

"Don't get excited," he says. "Everything's under control. You'll have your money on Monday."

"*Monday?!*" I blow my stack. "The deal was today!"

"Vince," he clucks, "I used to get angry like that till I went into therapy. You wanna cry and moan about what's not going to happen, or you wanna focus on what we really can do?"

"I did you a favor"—I'm seething—"and you hung me out to dry!"

"It's only a weekend," he says airily. "Who works weekends anymore? Can you honestly tell me your old man works weekends?"

"That's not the point—" I begin, but we get disconnected again. And when I call back, I get a busy signal.

That *idiot*. He knows better than anyone what Uncle Shank might do to him. How can he play games with something like this?

I keep telling myself it's not my fault. I've been trying to *help* the guy. If it wasn't for me, he would have been screwed a week ago. Dad's right. He's a total flake. I wash my hands of the whole rotten business.

But the image of Uncle Shank's pruning shears keeps haunting me. I see that shiny wet metal under our outdoor tap, and I don't care whose fault it is.

I drive to Long Beach—to the Silver Slipper, Ray's hangout.

He's unsympathetic. "You want to stay away from the business. Everybody respects that. But you can't be in for some things and out for others. Take my advice—let Jimmy worry about Jimmy. These things have a habit of working themselves out."

"And he'll be all right?"

He shrugs. "That's up to Jimmy. He knew what he was getting into when he took that money."

I figure I'd better just spell it out. "Can you guarantee that nothing's going to happen to his fingers?"

And he can't. I see it in his face. At that moment, I realize that I have to save Jimmy even if he can't save himself. But how?

The answer is simple. Six hundred bucks is how. Yeah, we've got money—*Dad's*. I get an allowance, but I've been blowing most of that on going out with Kendra. Practically zero in the bank and whatever's in my pocket—about twenty bucks and—what's this?

It's my emergency credit card, the one from Banco Commerciale de Tijuana. I could use it to get a six-hundred-dollar cash advance and pay what Jimmy owes Dad. Then, when Jimmy gives me the money on Monday, I'll head straight to the bank and make a payment on the account. It'll be back in there long before whoever's credit card it really is gets his next bill. By then it will look like a bank error: six hundred came out on Friday, and on Monday when the mistake was noticed, the six hundred was redeposited.

The teller gives me a funny look when he sees my Mexican credit card, but that isn't half of what I get from Dad when I hand over the six hundred that night. He's planing a chair leg, and he leans into it so hard that the thing snaps right in the clamp.

"From Jimmy Rat?"

"I told you he'd come through," I reply stubbornly.

I escape upstairs to the cover of the FBI listening devices before he can ask me any more questions.

[TWELVE]

I'M AMAZED AT HOW WELL Kendra and I still get along when
there's no talking. Movies quickly become our number-
two leisure-time activity. The only drawback is that, after
a couple of hours, the theater lights will come up and I'll
see the hurt and disappointment that's in her eyes almost
all the time now, or at least, all the time she's hanging
around me. Probably nobody else would even notice it. But
like a single minor chord in a symphony, it can change everything.

I don't mind it so much when she's mad at me. But the idea
that I'm letting her down is more than I can bear.

Yet, on the surface, it's a pretty good weekend. I see
Kendra both days, and the subject of dinner with her parents
never comes up.

That's why I'm totally caught off guard when I walk into
school on Monday and find myself facing a giant poster that
reads:

VOTE VINCE
AND KENDRA
FOR ROYAL COUPLE

Just as before, the letters are computer-generated. But this time the message has been broken into three lines, so it takes up the whole wall, from the top of the lockers clear up to the ceiling.

Again, the shock wears off and leaves only the mad. We've been through this already. How could she do it *again*?

I tear it down, but I can't reach the highest strip. So it still says VOTE VINCE. Eighteen hundred kids are entering the school while I stretch, jump, and try to scramble up the wall. Even *I* know that the sign couldn't possibly have garnered as much unwanted attention as I'm now giving it. A bunch of basketball players are watching me leap, and laughing their heads off. Any one of them could rip it down without so much as standing on tiptoe. Thanks a lot.

Mercifully, a somewhat friendly face, Alex, shows up. Actually, he's in a great mood. Alex's agreeability rises and falls in direct proportion to the degree of strife between Kendra and me. He gets on all fours, and I stand on his back and tear down the top piece. This earns us applause from the basketball players and a few other "fans."

"Thanks," I tell Alex. I really do appreciate his help. The guy is so image conscious. I mean, he lives in constant fear that he might do something to appear uncool in front of girls. He'll probably have nightmares for weeks about going down on his hands and knees in front of half the school.

"Vince, what are you going to do about this?" He indicates the crumpled sign in my hands.

I shake my head. "She swears it isn't her. I want to believe her except—who else could it be? Not that many people even know we're going out."

"Well, you'd better brace yourself," he warns me. "This isn't the only one. They're all over the school. I tore down a couple of smaller ones near my locker."

I sigh. "If I throw this in Kendra's face, guilty or innocent, that's going to be the end."

"If you guys get elected homecoming king and queen, that's going to be the end too," Alex points out.

I'm in despair. "It makes no sense, but I can't give her up, Alex. I don't know if it's having a girlfriend or her in particular. I realize it has to end sooner or later, but I have to hang on to it as long as I can."

I look at him as we walk to class. Because I know the guy so well, I can see that his teeth are clenched, which is something he only does when he's really upset. I understand instantly and feel bad. It was my little speech back there. I should have seen that all Alex would take out of it is that I'm happy, and he's missing out.

I make it through to lunch, only having to tear down one more poster. Now comes the hard part: keeping my big mouth shut when I see Kendra in the cafeteria.

I'm almost at my locker when I'm aware of someone's presence right behind me, and I suddenly feel the cold steel of a barrel thrust against the small of my back. I can't even begin to explain the thoughts that race through my head.

Ever since I was old enough to understand what my father does for a living, it has always been in the back of my mind that I could be a target one day. Somebody could want to get to Anthony Luca enough to attack his kid. I mean, the vending-machine business isn't *The Godfather.* There aren't wars; nobody goes to the mattresses; the uncles don't take turns crouched on our roof with rifles. But still, it's a tough line of work, and Dad makes enemies. In the wake of the Calabrese murder, Mom, Mira, and I went on a sudden, unplanned three-week tour of Norway. Tommy stayed, but Dad didn't let him buy a candy bar without a couple of the uncles driving him to the store.

My brother never got tired of messing with my head after that. He was always pointing out the assassin hiding in the bushes, the sniper in the window across the street, the kidnappers in that parked car over there. It just ratcheted up my paranoia level. Oh, I outgrew it. Or, at least, I repressed it. But now, standing in the hall with a gun against my spine, I realize that I've been waiting for this moment for half my life.

And then a menacing voice at my ear hisses, "Keep walking or your guts are gonna decorate that bulletin board!"

I wheel. "Are you out of your mind?"

Jimmy Rat stands there, laughing his stupid head off. The "gun" in his hand is a miniature flashlight key chain.

"Hey, Vince, you should see your face! I really had you going!"

"You had me 'going' in my pants!" I hiss. "If I dropped

dead of shock, you'd have a lot more to explain to my dad than six hundred lousy bucks."

He beams at me. "That's why I'm here, kid. There's a little surprise waiting in your locker. I slipped it in through the vent."

The money! I'm so relieved I almost forgive him. Now I can pay off the credit card and put this whole nightmare behind me.

I head for my locker. "Hey Jimmy, how'd you find out which one is mine?"

"I turned on a little of the old charm with the secretaries," he explains. "Told them I was your older brother."

"Yeah, right," I snort. "From Dad's first marriage during World War Two." I reach for the combination lock.

"Hey," says Jimmy. "That's not your locker."

"Sure it is," I reply. "678."

"No, it's 687!"

Can you believe it? Dumb *and* dyslexic. All rolled up into one unlovable, rodentlike package.

"Jimmy, you gave the money to the wrong guy!"

"Calm down, Vince," he tells me. "If your stress level is this high now, think what it'll be like when you get to be my age."

We move down the row to 687.

"Okay," I say. "This is Jolie's locker. I know her. When she comes, let me do all the talking. And pray she isn't absent today."

He gives me a superior smile, puts his ear up to the lock, and starts manipulating the dial.

I freak. "You can't break into a locker! This is a public school!"

"Where do you think I learned this?" he retorts. "Okay, when I count three, cough."

"But—"

"One . . . two . . ."

I manufacture a spasm, and, in that instant, Jimmy smacks the lock to pieces with his multipurpose flashlight key chain. The door swings open, and out falls a notebook, a makeup compact, and a grubby envelope marked VINSE. I guess in his school, where they teach you how to crack a locker, the instructional time is taken away from spelling class.

It's funny. I don't run, but I can't ever remember exiting school that fast.

Short, squat Jimmy matches me stride for stride. "Hey, Vince, don't you got no class to be going to?"

"I'm on lunch." Kendra, she's in the cafeteria, waiting for me. But this is more important. "I've got to run this money over to the bank. I borrowed to save your butt, Jimmy. You're welcome."

He's genuinely concerned. "Gee, you shouldn't have done that. You can get into a lot of trouble going into debt."

I roll my eyes. "What makes you say that?"

He misses the sarcasm. "I got this friend, Ed. Owns a real classy coffeehouse. You know, where those college pinheads pay four bucks to drink a cup of java that's half milk and sit on your great-grandmother's old velvet sofa. He makes money, but he's got a weakness for the ladies. And pretty soon he's in for a major chunk of change to some very heavy people.

I'm not mentioning any names, but we both know who's the heaviest around here."

"Dad," I say, almost to myself.

"Correct. And Ed's not feeling too good these days on account of your uncle No-Nose slamming that door on his head during their last meeting on the subject. Not that I blame your old man. Ed's stiffing him for almost a grand."

I stop him. "Listen, Jimmy. My father and his people do a lot of things I don't agree with. But it's out of my hands. I'm not in the business, and I'm never going to be. It was crazy for me even to get involved in your situation, and that's never going to happen again. It's not that I'm unsympathetic; it's just the way it has to be, okay?"

He puts an arm around my shoulders. "Don't worry about Ed. He's got options. He's got a great-aunt, ninety-three years old, over at St. Luke's on life support. Stands to inherit, like, thirty G's when she passes, which is maybe going to be soon."

I frown. "You mean because her condition is deteriorating, right?"

He shrugs. "You know how it is. She's been in a coma for months, and the doctors say she's never going to wake up. She's like a carrot, practically. But life support, that's just electricity, you see my point? I mean, people trip on wires all the time. Plugs get pulled out of the wall. It happens."

That's how I end up in a dark coffee bar in Soho, drinking a four-dollar cup of java that's half milk, sitting on my great-grandmother's velvet sofa, talking to Kendra on my cell phone.

"I'm in New York. I had to ditch the afternoon. Something came up."

"Are you okay, Vince? This doesn't have anything to do with all those posters about us, does it?"

"No. Just tear them down if you see any, okay? This is—it's nothing. What's new at school?"

"Jolie Fusco's locker got broken into, but she doesn't think anything was stolen."

Well, only six hundred bucks, but that was mine. "I can't really talk now. I'll call you when I get home."

I can almost see her reporter's face on the other end of the line. "Just tell me what it's all about, Vince. Maybe I can help."

"I'm fine. Talk to you later. Bye."

But I'm far from fine. For the second time, I'm deliberately interfering in my father's business, against my clearly stated sole purpose in life: to stay away from all that.

It's crazy. *I'm* crazy. Things like Jimmy's fingers, Ed's great-aunt—I'm sure they happen all the time. But I never knew about them before. Oh, how I wish I didn't know about them now! Things used to be so much easier. Sure, I figured Dad did some bad stuff, but it was all nonspecific. Nobody had a face or a name or a ninety-three-year-old great-aunt on life support.

Suddenly, I'm horrified at who I am and the kind of activities that finance the roof over my head, the clothes on my back, and the food I eat. Maybe that's why I'm here. Certainly it can't be for the financial well-being of the silk suit sitting in front of me.

Ed Mishkin is everything Jimmy Rat isn't: tall, good-looking, suave, with a triple-digit haircut and store-bought teeth. If it wasn't for the 360-degree bruise from the number Uncle No-Nose did on him, he could pass for a congressman. But he and Jimmy both have the same smile, an oily grin that oozes the words, "Can I interest you in a used car?"

"I really appreciate your help, Vince," he says with the kind of sincerity that could get a guy elected.

"I don't need your thanks," I mutter darkly. "I just want your aunt to die of natural causes. Let's finish this. You're short nine-fifty. I've got six hundred."

"I'm flat busted, Vince. I can come up with maybe a C."

I turn to Jimmy. "You've got to lend Ed two hundred and fifty bucks to get him past this."

Jimmy is appalled. "I just paid *you*! Plus my own vig comes up again soon."

I get mad. "I don't know why you two can't seem to budget. It's not brain surgery; it's fifth-grade math! But whatever the reason, the least you can do is help the other guy out. Then, a couple of weeks later, when *you're* the one in trouble, you've got help coming. There's double the chance that, at any given time, one of you guys will have a few extra bucks lying around."

And at that moment, I join a small and select group of people. I am now one of the very few to extract money—voluntarily—from Jimmy Rat. And I don't even need a hedge clipper to do it.

He digs a hand in his pocket and comes up with some crumpled bills. "I better get this back."

"The first six hundred pays my credit card," I tell them firmly.

Ed counts the money. "Hey, wait a minute. This is only a hundred and fifty. I'm still a hundred short."

I've had it. I walk up to the cash register, pop the till, and count out five twenties.

When I get home, Dad's out, and Tommy's hogging my computer.

"You've got five more minutes," I call from the bottom of the stairs. "I need to check my Web site."

Mom appears from the kitchen. "Thank goodness you're home. When your father gets back, we can sit down to dinner."

"Hello to you, too," I say sarcastically. "Come on, Mom. Surely a few thoughts pass through your head that aren't about food."

"Well," she deadpans back. "We could talk about what's keeping my seventeen-year-old son so busy night and day—and does she have a name."

Touché. "What's for dinner?" I mumble.

Come to think of it, I understand perfectly why her life seems to revolve around meals. Most of the time, the world spins out of her control, and God knows what her menfolk are up to. Dinner is that one shining moment where Captain Mom takes over the helm, and the good ship *Luca* goes where she steers it.

Even during the heavy heat that came after the Calabrese murder, with the cops and CNN dug into the lawn, I remember her serving pot roast and saying things like, "Vincent, what did you learn in school today?"

When any of us are in transit, you can tell Mom is off her game. The traffic report is blasting on the radio, and trust me, she doesn't care what roads are moving well. She's listening for accidents so she can stew over whether any of her loved ones are spread out all over the highway, bleeding.

"Mom, that pileup is in Jersey. What are you so worried about? Was Dad going to Jersey today?"

"How should I know where he's going?" she says in a wounded tone. "Your father doesn't provide me with an itinerary."

Actually, it's Agent Bite-Me he doesn't provide with an itinerary. Mom just happens to live in the same house as the FBI's microphones.

After producing food in mass quantities, worrying is her primary occupation. It's annoying, but I have to consider that her irrational fears are a cover-up for much more rational ones. Let's face it, how many guys in my father's position die at home in bed? Being his wife can't be easy.

When I finally get my hands on the computer, Tommy hangs around to watch me work on my Web site. Work may not be the word I'm looking for. It's more like sitting there in mute wonder. I now have over five hundred hits, and 187 ads in Meow Marketplace.

For sale: My cat Excelsior, age 3, knows how to quack. A real show-off. $500—T.S.

"How can a cat *quack*?" I yell at the screen.

"Must be a trained cat," puts in Tommy. "That's why he costs five hundred bucks."

"There is something very messed up going on here," I insist. "There are, like, twenty people who call their cat a prime minister! Or a movie star!"

"They live with *cats*," he explains reasonably. "They're freaks."

My head is spinning. "I mean, sure they think their cats are great! Cute! Furry! Not prime minister!"

"Maybe it's cat lingo," my brother reasons. "Every crowd has its own words for stuff. Like you Web site guys talk about getting hits, but in my business, a hit is something completely different."

The front door slams, and I listen for Mom to unload on Dad about being late. But she's sweet as pie, which usually means he has someone with him.

Tommy and I head for the atriumlike entranceway where Dad and Uncle No-Nose are taking off their jackets.

"Dad, I need to talk to you," I say. "Downstairs."

He raises his eyebrows but starts for the basement.

Uncle No-Nose shrugs back into his coat. "I should get going. I've got a few errands in the city."

"*No!*" I blurt out. Then, a little more composed, "I think you should hear this too, Uncle."

Now I've got his attention. My noninvolvement in the business is legendary among the uncles. It's the one rule that everybody follows—everybody except Dad and Tommy.

Downstairs, homemade rocking chairs await us. They were regular chairs in blueprints, but Anthony Luca's carpentry tends to have the same effect as a fun-house mirror. Dad sits in the best of the four, daring us to comment.

I hand over the nine hundred fifty dollars. "From Ed Mishkin," I explain.

Uncle No-Nose is confused. "Why'd he give it to *you*?"

"Vince is a big player now," Tommy says in disgust.

"I am not," I say heatedly. "I'm just helping the guy out because he's ready to pull the plug on his aunt's ventilator, and I don't think anyone should be that desperate."

"That guy's only desperate because he's a skirt chaser," snaps Tommy. "And that's an expensive hobby."

"I'll straighten this out," Uncle No-Nose promises.

"You've got your money," I interject. "What difference how it comes to you?"

Tommy looks at me. "These guys you love so much—you know they're dirtbags, right?"

Uncle No-Nose turns to my father, trying to gauge the boss's opinion on all this. Smarter people than No-Nose have tried and failed to read Anthony Luca. And I include myself and a whole lot of U.S. attorneys on that list.

Finally, my father speaks. "You know I'm interested in this, Vince. You're a man now, and the choices you make show the world who you are. So tell me, is this the real you? Are you dedicating your brains to baby-sitting a couple of lowlifes?"

"You've got to let me do this," I insist. "It's important to me."

"They're playing you like a piano!" Tommy roars.

"Then it's my decision who I get played by," I say stubbornly.

Dad speaks to Uncle No-Nose first. "Nose, you get a pass on Ed Mishkin for a while. However bad my son screws it up, it's no reflection on you. And your points stay the same."

Uncle No-Nose looks surprised. "You got it, Tony. But it doesn't make any sense."

"No kidding," Dad sighs. To me he says, "Go find yourself. And don't take too long doing it."

[THIRTEEN]

OF ALL **K**ENDRA'S GOOD QUALITIES, this has to be number one: she never holds it against Alex that he can't stand her. Think about it. He hates her for no other reason than the fact that she's my girlfriend. Which means there's nothing she can do short of breaking up with me that will make him like her any better. It's a classic no-win situation. Yet while she finds plenty to complain about where I'm concerned, she never utters a single word against Alex.

In fact, she tries really hard not to leave him out of things. She invites him along to movies and to hang out with us at the mall. And he always accepts, which is pretty weird, because every minute he spends with us, he's totally miserable. I know it, and he knows I know it.

"If you're not having fun, *stay home!*"

He glares at me. "You'd like that, wouldn't you?"

"No!" I insist. "We invited you. We want you to come. But if you hate it—"

"There's nothing to do at home," he grumbles.

Next Christmas, I should buy him a satellite dish.

Kendra bends over backward to be nice to the guy. She even lets him listen to her K-Bytes karaoke tapes, which he professes to love. I know for a fact that he made a copy for himself and dubbed in thirty minutes of strategically placed burps and raspberries. I saw the cassette cover. In between *K* and *Bytes*, he scribbled the word *really*.

This is my best friend in the world. What am I supposed to do? He's not going to change, and I'm not going to dump Kendra. Stalemate.

So we're in the multiplex on Saturday. Kendra and I are watching the movie while Alex spits Gummi Bears at the screen because he hates Gwyneth Paltrow almost as much as he hates Kendra.

The mall always seems extra bright after two hours in the dark. We're standing there, squinting in the light, when a voice from above calls, "Hi, honey."

Kendra turns and looks up at the mezzanine. "Hi, Daddy."

My bones turn to Jell-O. A man is heading toward the elevator on the upper level where the offices are. Her father. Agent Bite-Me.

My voice, when I can finally access it, sounds like a two-year-old with a stomachache. "He's coming *here*?"

Kendra nods. "He had a dentist appointment, so I thought we might run into each other."

"No!" I croak. I catch a glimpse of Alex, who's smiling for the first time in days.

Kendra gapes at me. "Vince, what's the problem? You got something against a free cup of coffee?"

The elevator is on its way down. "We talked about this!" I rasp.

Storm clouds are gathering on her brow. "This isn't the same thing," she says sharply. "This is 'How's it going?' and maybe ten minutes over coffee. It won't kill you."

The elevator stops at the mall level. "I can't meet him."

"What, is there another girl somewhere?" she demands.

"You've got it all wrong—"

"You're *never* going to admit we're together!"

"No—"

But my feeble protests are no match for the Wrath of Kendra. "You must have a screw loose!" she exclaims. "If you can't do this, you and I are through as of this second! Give me one good reason why you can't shake hands and introduce yourself to my dad!"

Agent Bite-Me is off the elevator now, threading his way through the shoppers toward us. I'm out of options. Considering that I always knew this moment would come eventually, I'm shocked, bewildered, and panicked. It's the proverbial rock and a hard place. I'm dead.

And then it just comes pouring out: "My father is Anthony Luca. He's a suspected Mob boss, and your dad has been trying to put him in jail for the past five years!"

If I whacked her upside the head with a dead fish, she couldn't look more thunderstruck. As we stand there, staring at each other, I realize that I have absolutely no idea what's going to happen next. Over the past month and a half, I've come to know practically everything about this girl. But I don't have a clue what she's going to do now.

Suddenly, she wheels away from me, pulling Alex with her, and calls, "Over here, Dad. I want you to meet someone."

If that's not a cue, I don't know what is. I melt into the crowd and hide behind the shirt rack in Banana Republic.

I hang around, sidling and spying, so much that mall security is eyeing me. I figure if those dummies notice me, I shouldn't take my chances with an FBI agent. I wander around the far side of the mall.

I'm freaking out. There are so many things that could go wrong here that I can't even count them all. Kendra could hate me now. She could be confessing everything to her father this very minute. Or worse, Alex could spill the beans accidentally on purpose, just because he can't stand it that I've got a girlfriend and he doesn't.

I struggle to kill time. There's a pet shop just off the food court, and I'm fascinated by a kitten in the window. The card reads: 6-WK-OLD CALICO, ALL SHOTS. Not a word about a political career or a future in the entertainment industry. How come there aren't any cats like this on my Web site?

Out of the corner of my eye, I catch sight of Alex storming through the mall.

"Hey, wait!"

A burst of speed, and I'm in his path. "What happened? How did it go?"

"Oh, it was a barrel of laughs!" he spits back at me. "I've got the total green light to date his daughter. What's wrong with that picture?"

"How's Kendra?"

"How should I know?" he says bitterly. "I was too busy

convincing her father what a fine upstanding young man I am. Story of my life. The parents all love me. It's their daughters who hate my guts!"

"*Al-ex!*"

"She's in the bathroom. The coast is clear. Her dad's gone home. I'm going to do the same, not that anybody cares."

I start down the corridor to the washrooms. "I owe you," I toss over my shoulder.

"You and the rest of the world," I hear him retort.

I make up my mind that if she won't come out, I'm going into the ladies' room to get her. That should give mall security something to think about. But she does come out and stops dead in the doorway, gawking at me with an intensity that's almost scary. I stare back, trying to decode her expression. Is it over?

And then she hurls herself at me and grabs me, kissing me so hard that we stagger into the pay phone on the opposite wall. I recover and get with the program, but this is more than just a kiss and make up. This is frantic, passionate. Our teeth grind together, but we don't care. Our one purpose is to get close, really close. And there's an urgency to it that transcends all other priorities.

We spin off the cinder-block wall and knock into a stack of WET FLOOR signs that go down like dominoes to the terrazzo.

"I don't care who your father is!" she breathes into my mouth.

"I don't care who *your* father is!" I breathe back.

Unbelievable. Turns out Kendra thinks we're some kind

of cops-and-robbers Romeo and Juliet—star-crossed lovers from families that are mortal enemies. And I'm not much for locker-room talk, but I've got to say that it ratchets up the intensity level of our relationship about five hundred percent. Hey, if I knew this was going to happen, I would have told her about Anthony Luca on day one.

We finally talk it out in a secluded parking spot on Bryce Beach, the very scene of my debacle with Angela O'Bannon. It's freezing at the shore, but we're generating our own heat, and the windows are too steamed up for us to bother with the view.

She says, "I don't even think I know what a Mob boss does." Her head is on my shoulder, and she twists to look up at me. "How pathetic is that for an agent's daughter to be so naïve?"

"Not pathetic, lucky," I tell her. "I'd give anything to go back to the days when my father was the best dad in the world, with no asterisks."

"I'm sick of being Little Miss Innocent," she says suddenly. "Give me the job description. What is it that's so important that my father has to put in fourteen-hour days and run himself into the ground?"

I shake my head. "I'm the low man on the totem pole at our house. There's only one thing I have control over: I have nothing to do with Dad's business. That's the way I stay me in our family."

All at once, so many things can make sense between us: my phony jobs; the real reason I quit the football team; why I don't park near her door; why I call her on a cell phone.

She seems amazed that the FBI is allowed to bug our house.

"The point is, you can't ever come over," I explain. "Even if I can bluff you past my folks, your dad would recognize your voice on the surveillance tapes."

"What if we give you a fake name?" Kendra suggests thoughtfully. "Then I could 'break up' with Alex and introduce you as Bernie or somebody."

"No good," I sigh. "Your father knows my face. The FBI watches the place, too. They even took pictures at my sister's wedding. Dad asked them to make up a special album, but it didn't go over very well."

She looks determined. "We can't judge them, Vince. Your side or mine. We're going to have to keep out of it and let them do what they do. We just have to stay focused on *us*."

I agree with her. But my mind is already wandering to the rumors of an inside man in the Luca organization. If that man exists, and Agent Bite-Me is about to bring an indictment against my father, how will I feel about Kendra then?

[FOURTEEN]

I'M STARTING TO EARN A REPUTATION around school as the guy
who really doesn't want to be Homecoming King. People get
that impression from the cursing and muttering I do every
time I tear down another Vince-and-Kendra poster.

Yes, the posters are still coming, more than there ever
were before. There's even a group of nitwit football players
who think it's funny to shake me down over it.

"Hey, Luca," one of them will call, "give us twenty bucks
or we'll all vote for you!" And everybody cracks up laughing.

If we win, my first action as Homecoming King will be to
demand a recount.

There's one bright spot. At least now I know Kendra isn't
doing it.

Alex disagrees. "Don't be so sure, Vince. Chicks get off on
this Homecoming stuff."

"Impossible," I say flatly. "It would ruin everything."

"It's a psychological thing with women," he goes on
reasonably. "On the one hand, there's logic. But pulling

from the other side is an irresistible desire to be queen."

My life may be in turmoil. But it's going to have to get a lot worse before I'm taking advice about women's irresistible desires from MisterFerrariDriver.

Speaking of our Web sites, ILuvMyCat has moved into second place on the hit parade and is gaining fast on CyberPharaoh. I'm thrilled when I get a second message on Cat Tales, but it turns out to be the same eighty-five-year-old talking about her dear departed Fluffy again.

Fluffy: a good name for a cat. Ides of March: not such a good name.

Prime ministers. Movie Stars. Quackers. Eight Balls. Inky cats. Cats that'll have you in seventh heaven. What are the odds that more than one person takes his pet to a toga party? How about fourteen? I counted yesterday.

I don't know what to do. Alerting the police would be too extreme, especially for a Luca. Besides, they'll think I'm nuts. So I bring in the next-best thing: a real FBI agent's daughter. Kendra applies her considerable talents as an investigative reporter to my case.

"Well, obviously these aren't real ads," she says after two minutes.

"How can you be sure?"

She rolls her eyes at me. "Vince, for five hundred bucks you can get a cat with a pedigree that stretches back to the saber-toothed tiger, not a Heinz fifty-seven whose only claim to fame is that he can quack. And these names—they're not even real names. Just phrases or expressions: Military Intelligence or I Love a Parade."

I can't help but marvel at the logical, methodical way her mind works. Maybe it's true that the apple doesn't fall very far from the tree—although, in my case, that's a pretty scary thought. The last person I want to be like is Anthony Luca.

She looks up from the monitor to face me in the cramped library cubicle. "Could it be a hacker?"

I shake my head. "There's no hacking involved. Anybody with a computer can place ads on the site."

"A joker, then," she suggests. "Somebody from the class. How about Alex? He's got a pretty warped sense of humor."

"It still wouldn't explain the traffic," I tell her. "I've got seven hundred hits. No way all that's coming from a single user."

"There's only one other thing those ads could be," she muses. "Coded messages."

"Aw, come on!" I explode.

"I'm serious." She swivels the screen so I can see it. "Each ad has two numbers, a dollar amount and a lower number: *a real eight ball, four on the floor, seventh heaven.* Then there are key words that come up again and again: *quack, toga party, prime minister—*"

I'm horrified. "But that's crazy! This is real life, not a Tom Clancy novel!"

I take her theory to Mr. Mullinicks, mostly because I'm hoping he'll laugh in my face. But he sticks to his guns, insisting that whatever's happening on ILuvMyCat, it's my problem. The other kids agree that something weird is going on. But they've got their own Web sites to worry about.

As for Tommy, he doesn't see anything strange at all. The

one good thing to come out of New Media class is the interest all this has kindled in my brother. He even found himself a computer and set it up in his apartment in the city. I got my first e-mail from him last night:

**hey vince how's it going write me back
so I know this crap works tommy**

Tommy's computer apparently has no punctuation marks or capital letters.

Of course, I see the guy practically every day. So by the time I retrieve that message, he's standing right there beside me. He practically shrieks with delight when his words pop onto the screen. It's like taking a four-year-old to Disney World.

Mom appears in the doorway, a heaping tray of s'mores in her hands. "Look at you two, working that space-age gizmo like a couple of professors."

My mother loves to watch us with our heads together at the computer. It helps her see her family as the wholesome folks she deludes herself into believing we are.

"Who's dying?" I ask suspiciously. S'mores are Mom's version of first aid. She only makes them for incoming wounded.

"No one, smart guy," she retorts. "Your uncle Cosimo dropped by, poor man. His gout is acting up again."

I grimace. Uncle Cosimo's last attack of "gout" came via a shotgun full of rock salt as he was hotwiring a Range Rover.

Tommy heads for the stairs. "I'd better talk to him."

I watch as he disappears to take care of business. I'll never change my brother, I realize. But I'm glad I was able to turn him on to something that's actually legal, although I'm willing to bet that his computer was liberated rather than bought and paid for.

To be honest, I'm spending less and less time on any kind of schoolwork these days, because I've got a new project that's occupying all my powers of reasoning. There must be some way for Jimmy Rat and Ed Mishkin to get back on track with their debts, while at the same time paying me the six hundred dollars I owe on my/Dad's/somebody's credit card.

The thing is, Jimmy and Ed both seem to make plenty of money. But since they pay my dad only once a month, they always manage to blow all their cash so there's not enough left when the Uncles come around to collect. Ed apparently spends everything on women, and Jimmy Rat? Who knows what happens to his money? He clearly isn't spending it on fine clothes and good grooming, and definitely not on deodorant.

Basically, these two don't need a wiseguy; they need a financial planner. And so long as I'm going to lose sleep over Jimmy's fingers and Ed's great-aunt, I guess it has to be me.

The first problem is expecting these blockheads to think ahead a whole month. So I calculate the amount each man has to take out of his cash register every night and not touch. From there, I add in an installment plan so that I get my six hundred back, and Ed returns the one-fifty I made Jimmy lend him last week. Then comes the tricky part. I fix it so that

Ed overpays Jimmy for the first two weeks when Jimmy's tab is coming due, and vice versa after that.

I'm pretty proud of myself by the time I put it on an Excel spreadsheet and print it out. Then I call up Jimmy. All this time I'm being Thank-you–PaineWebber, I forget that Jimmy is about as convenient to reach as Saddam Hussein. Ed's easier to get on the line because he's usually waiting for a call from a lady friend. I know this because he always answers "Hey, there, hot stuff."

I tell Ed about my new system, but he doesn't even seem interested. Then he starts talking about a movie he saw!

I remember something Tommy says: nobody can ignore you when you're standing on their neck. Well, I'm not going to hurt anyone, but I'm also not going to be ignored.

I interrupt Ed's graphic description of the leading lady's lingerie. "Listen, Ed. I'm coming down there tomorrow after school. If you and Jimmy don't show up, I'm washing my hands of both of you." I slam down the phone.

That night I show Dad my payment plan spreadsheet. He laughs so hard that he mauls an expensive piece of walnut on the table saw.

I'm deeply wounded. "What's so funny?"

Tommy isn't as amused. "You know how that's going to help a guy like Jimmy Rat? He'll save money on toilet paper, that's all."

Ray is the kindest of the three, but even he isn't very encouraging. "You've got a good heart, kid, but you're wasting your time. These guys could start the month with Fort

Knox in their pockets and be tapped out by the fifteenth."

"You're wrong," I say defensively, "and I'll prove it."

All the way through bumper-to-bumper traffic into the city, my mind is in Kendra's basement, where I would be if it wasn't for this meeting. To stay focused, I keep glancing over at the passenger seat where my spreadsheets sit rolled up and waiting, like blueprints for a better life for those two idiots. It takes an hour and a half to creep into Manhattan and another twenty minutes to park.

Frankly, I'm pleasantly surprised to find Jimmy and Ed huddled in a corner booth at Java Grotto, Ed's place.

I hand out the spreadsheets and say my piece, going into real detail about exactly how it has to work. Amazingly, they follow me. They're money guys, businessmen.

There's a long silence when I'm done, and then Jimmy says, "No can do, Vince."

I'm shocked. "What do you mean, no can do? You don't have a choice. Don't you know what the alternative is?"

Ed clears his throat. "Hey, Vince, how about a latte on the house?"

"No!" I exclaim. "This isn't about coffee! And nothing should be on the house until you straighten out your finances!"

Jimmy pipes up. "We're real grateful for all your help. In fact"—he rolls up the spreadsheet and slips a rubber band on it—"I like this so much that I'm going to frame it and hang it on my wall."

I almost blow a gasket. "Don't patronize me! You don't

like my way? Fine, do it your way! How much money have you saved up so far?"

They stare at me.

"*None?*" I howl. "*Nothing?* What are you doing—flushing it down the toilet?"

"See, the thing is," says Jimmy, "there's stuff about us you don't know. A few months ago me and Ed became investors in an establishment."

"What kind of establishment?" I ask suspiciously.

"It's in the entertainment industry," Ed supplies. "Adult entertainment."

"A strip joint," I conclude.

"Correct," says Jimmy. "I see you're a man of the world, Vince. We bought into the Platinum Coast up on Thirty-Ninth. Used to be the Wiggle Lounge before the mayor's boys shut it down on account of too much wiggling and not enough lounging. Real classy place."

"So what's the problem?" I demand. "Use the profits from the Platinum Coast to help pay my dad."

"There *are* no profits," Ed breaks in. "The place is eating money right now. And Boaz—he's our partner—he keeps coming to us to kick in more."

I shrug. "Tell him no."

"But we've got so much invested already!" Jimmy whines. "If we let it fold, we lose everything!"

"It's still better than throwing good money after bad," I argue.

"But these places are gold mines," Ed groans. "If we could ever get the Coast off the ground, we'd be rolling in cash! It's been nothing but headaches so far—beefs with the cops, with the liquor license, with the landlord. We've spent more time closed than open. Once that gets straightened out—"

Jimmy grabs my arm. "Come see the place, Vince!"

I pull myself free. "Why?"

"It's such a thing of beauty! Once you see it, you'll understand why we can't let it go."

"It's a strip joint!" I exclaim.

"Not a strip joint," protests Jimmy. "A gentleman's club, where prominent men of this community can go after a hard day's work to relax and unwind."

"And the chicks are smokin'!" adds Ed.

I think it over. Of course I don't want to see this cesspool. But I guess I'm sort of their financial advisor. And this is an asset. Someday their equity in this place could be a bargaining chip to trade for these guys' kneecaps.

They're right. I'd better go check it out.

We take my car. That way I can hustle those two into a cab and zip right out the Midtown Tunnel after I've viewed this objet d'art. I'm dying to rush right home and take a shower. Dealing with Jimmy and Ed makes me feel like I've been dipped in cooking oil.

Even in broad daylight, I can see the place glowing half a block away. That's where the money's going, to pay the electric bill. I find a parking space right across the street, and we sit staring, mesmerized by the chaser lights and the pink neon. I can see us reflected in the mirrored doors, Jimmy, Ed, and me. What in God's name am I doing in this place with these people?

"Ain't it a sight?" raves Jimmy.

"A sight and a half," I agree.

"Come on, we'll show you the inside."

"Wait a minute," I protest. "I'm underage."

"Nobody's going to card you," laughs Ed. "You're with us."

"Besides," adds Jimmy, "you've got to meet Boaz. Maybe you can straighten him out. You know, get him to stop bleeding us."

I quail. "*Me?* I'm a high-school kid! What could I possibly say to a guy who runs a place like this?"

"Well, for starters," says Ed, "you can tell him your name."

"Vince?" I echo, bewildered. And then it becomes clear. Teenager or not, my last name is Luca. Jimmy and Ed are hoping that this Boaz person will take one look at me and assume I speak for my dad.

I'm really mad. "You planned this!" I accuse. "I wondered why you showed up just because I asked you to! You're not interested in budgeting! You just want me to convince this guy you're under my father's protection!"

"Aw, Vince," pleads Jimmy, "it's not like that."

"It's *exactly* like that! Well, I won't do it! What's more, if you guys go in there and tell them I'm with you, I'm going to make sure my dad knows you're using his name when you've got no right!"

Well, that gets a reaction. I've never heard so much apologizing in my life. The two of them scramble out of my Mazda and hotfoot it past the velvet rope into the club. Just before the door swings shut, I catch a quick glimpse of a lone dancer wrapped around a shiny silver pole. The silhouette of her figure keeps me sitting there, hanging out the car window, long after the door closes. I guess I'm hoping it'll open again and give me another look.

It does, a minute later. And this time I don't even see my dancer, because out onto the red carpet step three of the most beautiful women I've ever seen. Even through baseball caps and bulky sweatshirts, it's obvious they're knockouts. Good old Ed was right about one thing: The ladies of the Platinum Coast really are smokin'.

Then one of them looks right at me, and calls, "Vince?"

I almost tumble out the car window. But then I recognize her. It's Cece, my "present" from Tommy. She remembers me! Then again, she probably doesn't run into too many guys who turn her down.

I get out of the car and move to shake her hand; she hugs me. I'm uncomfortable at first. But she says, "No hard feelings, right?" and the awkwardness passes.

"You dance here?" I ask.

She shakes her head. "I'm not a dancer. I work my appointments out of the office. It's not a real club, you know."

Confused, I motion toward the mirrored door. "There's a girl onstage—"

"That's just for show," Cece assures me. "Boaz and Rafe move swag in and out of the back, and a lot of us girls take our calls here. That's all there is."

It's hard to concentrate with her standing so close, but I think I get the message. "Are you saying this place is a front?"

"Jeez, no!" she exclaims. "This is Boaz's masterpiece, his biggest score. He and Rafe sold about seven hundred percent of the club to silent partners. And they're milking them dry, the poor dumb jerks." She stares at me. "Are you okay, Vince? You're white as a sheet."

"I—I'll give your regards to Tommy." On wobbly legs I climb back in the car. I'm three blocks away before I realize I'm going in the wrong direction, heading for New Jersey instead of Long Island. Turning around is an act that requires almost more than I can give. I can't make the simplest decisions. Should I warn Jimmy and Ed that they're getting scammed? Of course! So how come I'm driving away? It's as if I think that by putting distance between me and the Platinum Coast, I can remove myself from this whole sick business.

I go through the Midtown Tunnel, but pull over just past the tolls. If I drive on the expressway in this state of mind, I'll be in grave danger of wrapping myself around a telephone pole.

My brain is in overdrive, figuring angles like a computer analyzing thousands of permutations. How stupid I was to think I could get those two over a hump and back on their feet again. They'll never get square. Even if they cut off Boaz, the loss of their investment and the interest on the debts they incurred to make it will drag them under. And what does that mean? For starters, I can kiss the six hundred good-bye, but that's not what bothers me. It's Jimmy and Ed. They might be able to bluff through a month here, a month there. But in the long run, the cards are stacked against them. And they're going to pay with their bones and fingers, which is appalling enough. But one of these days, they're going to pay with their lives!

I pull back into traffic, calmer, but far from calm. If I ever needed proof that the vending-machine business isn't for me, here it is. I'm barely grazing the surface, and I'm already in way over my head. There's only one person with a prayer of being able to sort all this out.

When I pull up in front of our house, there's a big limo parked on the circular drive, and Dad, Tommy, and Ray are climbing into the back.

I hit the ground running. "Dad! . . . *Dad!*"

My father pauses. "I've got a meeting, Vince. Mom's keeping some ziti hot for you."

"Dad, just give me a minute!"

"You okay, Vince?" calls Tommy from the car. "You don't look so hot."

I just blurt it all out. "Jimmy and Ed are getting ripped off! They're never going to be able to pay back that money!"

"That's not my business," my father says firmly. "And it's definitely not yours."

"How can you say that?" I explode. "Of course it's your business! You're never going to get paid! And you're going to have to do God knows what because of it!"

My father fixes me with the Luca stare, which shuts me up in a hurry. "I don't want to hear it. And I definitely don't want it hollered all over the neighborhood. Do you think you're the first scared kid to come to me wild-eyed and babbling like this? I've seen it a million times, and it always means the same thing: something you're arrogant enough to think you've got under control is starting to get away from you."

"You're my *father*!" I manage. "Help me!"

"I *am* helping you," he barks, "if you'd pull your head out of your butt long enough to see it! I cut you a lot of slack, Vince, because I was trying to let you find your own direction. It stops today. Listen good: starting now, you don't talk to Jimmy Rat and that Ed guy. And I'm going to pass the word on to them that they don't go anywhere near you."

"You're signing their death warrants!"

But Dad doesn't answer. In his opinion, the law has been laid down and the issue is closed.

I hear Ray's voice: "Is it okay if I catch up with you guys in my own car?"

"Sure, why not?" my father says wearily. "Go bang *your* head against a brick wall for a while."

Ray gets out of the stretch, and my dad climbs in. As we watch the limo drive off, he puts an arm around my shoulders.

"Friendly piece of advice. Never say 'warrant' to your old man."

I laugh, but I feel like I'm on the verge of crying. "It's not funny."

"No, it's not," he agrees solemnly. "It's business."

"Business sucks."

He's kind but firm. "Maybe your father's right to be worried about you, Vince. You don't know the difference between work and play. Work is hard. It takes all day, and nobody questions the fact that some people aren't always happy with the results. You think it's different in any other business? You think on Wall Street, if you screw up, you don't get fired?"

"Fired, yeah," I reply. "Nobody gets killed."

"You don't know for sure that anybody's going to get killed here either," he reminds me. "Your old man's a tough guy, but he's not a monster. He's happiest when everyone gets paid, and your uncles sit around all day playing cards."

"But he's *not* going to get paid."

Ray shrugs. "There's probably going to be unrest in East Bumwipe tomorrow. I don't like it, but you don't see me getting on a plane to try to stop it. There are a million things you can change and a million things you can't. You're a seventeen-year-old kid with a big future. You're going to college next year. You've got a great girlfriend—that's still going on, right?"

I nod. "It's a little complicated, but nothing I can't handle."

"*That's* what you should be focusing on. Tell you what. I know this guy, owns a restaurant down in Lido. Real romantic, right on the water. Take her there tomorrow night. I'll set the whole thing up."

"You're buying me off."

"Women love this place," he persists. "Trust me."

"Now you sound like Alex."

"Except *I* can get a date," he reminds me.

"All right." I clap him on the shoulder. "Thanks, Ray."

"Anytime. Hey, I've got to fly. Can't keep the boss waiting."

I almost ask it then, the question that's been on my mind

ever since I was old enough to understand that the vending-machine business isn't really about vending machines. It's true. I'm seventeen. I've got my whole life in front of me. Ray Francione was my age once too. What would make a stand-up guy like him choose to become a gangster?

Was it the money? The women? A rebellious streak? Who knows what makes a person choose a career outside the law?

My father says it was his first paycheck that did it for him. Supposedly, Dad took one look at the deductions for tax and Social Security and decided Uncle Sam was shaking him down. Now *he's* a kind of government, and in his world, a percentage of everything goes to him. As far as he's concerned, he just turned the tables on a raw deal. It's no small accomplishment. Lawyers, doctors, bankers—Dad's as sharp as the best of them. He could have been anything.

Could have been . . .

Is there really any point to applying those three words to Anthony Luca and the people who work for him? They make their choices and that's it. For all I know, with the right agent, Uncle Pampers might have been Garth Brooks. Instead, he keeps undertakers in business.

Choices.

I hope I make the right ones.

[FIFTEEN]

KENDRA AND I GET THE IDEA to make a big thing out of Ray's dinner. Get dressed up, go early, stay late, the whole nine yards.

I've resolved to give my father the silent treatment over Jimmy and Ed. Wouldn't you know it—I can't figure out how to tie my tie. Tommy doesn't have a clue. Neither does Mom. Guess who that leaves.

I find Dad downstairs at the wood lathe, hollowing a spinning bowl with a chisel that looks like a toothpick in his beefy hands. I stifle a laugh. The vending-machine king of New York is sawdust from head to toe.

I can't resist. "The yeti lives!" I cry.

He shuts off the machine. "How'd you like to visit the Himalayas?" he growls. "One-way trip."

My smile disappears. Threats from my father, even joking ones, aren't funny anymore. They probably never were.

"Help me with my tie?" I ask.

He takes a step toward me, and a blizzard of wood

shavings is airborne. "I'll meet you upstairs," he says. "I might have to turn the Shop-Vac on myself."

When we finally get to the tie, he has to stand behind me, reaching around my shoulders, because he can't form the knot mirror image. "When did you get so tall, kid?"

I step away from him. "Thanks," I mumble.

"I think it's great of Ray to set this up for you," he says. A peace offering, I think. He sounds uncomfortable. Anthony Luca doesn't have to mend fences very often. It's usually the other guy's problem to make it up to him. "I hope I get to meet your girl someday."

"Maybe you will," I say lamely. But in reality, the only way I can see that happening is if his racketeering trial happens to fall on Take Your Daughter to Work Day. I feel instantly guilty for the thought. He's my father, and I can't bear the idea of him going to prison.

"You were right all along," he continues. "The Life isn't for you. I never should have let you get involved in that thing."

That *thing*. Classic Anthony Luca. When we're not in the basement, and the FBI might be listening, there are no specifics in the Luca house. It's all "things," "situations," sometimes "whatchamacallits." "Problems," too, although problems can also be people. Before he became a corpse, Calabrese was a problem.

I don't give Dad the satisfaction of an answer. I am involved in this *thing*, and nobody can undo that, not even the great Anthony Luca.

He sure can make it difficult, though. I spend the whole

day trying to call Jimmy Rat with no success. I do manage to reach Ed on the bimbo hotline, but the instant he hears my voice, he freaks. "Jeez, Vince, ya trying to get me killed?" Slam.

My father's edicts have a way of hitting the streets in record time, and I don't doubt that Uncle No-Nose is very effective at getting his point across.

Dad takes one last stab at making up. "I know you're mad, Vince. But one day you'll see that this is what's best for all of us."

For him, maybe. Possibly even for me. But I can't imagine any way this could work to the benefit of Jimmy Rat and Ed Mishkin.

I pick Kendra up just a block away from her front door, carefully tucked behind a stand of foliage. I reflect that I'll need a new hiding place soon. The trees have lost a lot of leaves, an occupational hazard of dating in late October. In the winter, this spot will be in the direct line of vision of Kendra's upstairs hall window.

I see her legs first, longer than I remember, moving down the sidewalk. She comes into view from south to north: mini-skirt, top, et cetera. By the time her face appears, I'm craning my neck like a construction worker. Kendra is one of those low-maintenance girls who always manage to look good with almost no effort. For her, doing her hair means toweling it dry. I've never seen her like this before, dressed up, made up, hair up. She's so—up!

I'm proud. I know that's a shallow way to be, and very Luca. In the vending-machine business, beauty is less than skin deep; it's actually skin. But I can't help myself. I, who have rubbed elbows (and almost more than that) with the likes of Cece and therefore know what I'm talking about, have a hot girlfriend. Maybe that makes me no better than Ed Mishkin, but it feels great and I don't care.

I watch her fold those legs into my passenger seat. "You look nice," I say, understatement of the millennium.

"You too."

And we laugh like idiots and drive off, happier than anybody has the right to be.

The restaurant, Topsiders, is built right out onto a pier, with a perfect view of the water through twenty-foot-high glass panels. The place is crowded, but they're expecting us at the desk. So while everybody else waits for tables, the maitre d' whisks us off to the best seats in the house, right by the window.

She's amazed, but I'm quite used to this treatment. You think Anthony Luca ever waits for a table? I always used to hate our "special status." But tonight I see it through Kendra's eyes, and I'm not even embarrassed to admit I'm psyched.

"Connections," I reply to her amazed look.

She complains about being naïve, but it's something I really like about her. It never occurs to her that these are the very same kind of connections that her father spends his days investigating.

The dinner is a blur. It's funny, I can go on forever about the bad things, the things that go wrong, like Angela O'Bannon, and my Web site, and this mess with Jimmy and Ed. But about a perfect night with Kendra, I don't have much to say. Maybe I just can't think of a bunch of flowery words to describe how the moon is right. But it is, shining full, casting a silvery trail along the water. I remember great food, but food isn't what's important. I have a very clear recollection of Ray checking up on us. He doesn't even say hi—doesn't want to intrude, I guess. I catch a quick glimpse of him, peering through the potted palms, making sure our table is just right, and we're having a good time. I look back a moment later, and he's gone.

I almost run after him. I want to introduce him to Kendra so we can thank him. Then I realize that's not Ray's way. He's a terrific guy, the best. But he likes to stay under the radar screen. Even in Dad's organization, where he's a rising star, he keeps a low profile, content to baby-sit my brother rather than go for the big money and the glitz. He wouldn't want us to make a scene. But just seeing him there for a split second leaves me with a very warm feeling.

Maybe that's why this night is so spectacular for me. How many times can you sit back and say, *This is me.* When I picture my life exactly the way I want it to be, I'm right here, right now. And Kendra Bightly is the girl sitting across from me.

I can't bring myself to tell her that she's the best thing that's ever happened to me, and I love her. I want to. I can feel myself actually starting to do it a couple of times. But I'm a Luca. My DNA is engineered for scratching myself in a sleeveless undershirt, not sharing my emotions. Still, just the fact that those words crossed my mind—the big three—that's huge.

Afterward, when I drop her off, I can't even make it all the way home before I need to hear her voice again. But when I turn on my cell phone, the service has been shut off.

Ray warned me about this. Cloned phones don't last forever. Eventually, the company figures out that you're bootlegging the service. Pretty soon the police will trace the number. They're probably trying already.

Following Ray's instructions, I drive to the beach and pitch my cell into the ocean.

The thing about cell phones is, you don't realize how much you need them until they're gone. I've never felt so out of touch. I try Kendra from a payphone a few times, but one of her parents always answers, so I hang up. I wonder if she's trying to call me and getting a message that the number is out of service. I even do a few drive-bys of her house, but she's not outside, and I can't catch her attention in a window.

Ray's nowhere to be found. Tommy says Jersey, but I run into Uncle Exit, who mentions something about a fishing trip with Primo out east. Either way, I'm stuck with Alex, and when he finds out why I'm free to hang around, he isn't flattered.

Because I see Alex every day at school, I never realized just how out of touch with the guy I've become. He's turning into an embittered hermit, sequestered in his darkened room, chain-watching a never-ending *Star Trek* marathon. The guy has every single episode on video, and I'm talking classic Trek: *The Next Generation, Deep Space Nine, Voyager,* and all the movies.

"You know," I begin carefully while *The Search for Spock* plays in the background, "you've got to snap out of it."

His eyes never leave the screen. "Snap out of what?"

I take in the room. His computer is half buried in dirty clothes, and there are thirty-seven unopened messages on MisterFerrariDriver. His fish tank is so murky that the goldfish are gray, wraithlike figures. His prize Chia Pet is stone dead. I'm sure he hasn't shaved in weeks, which isn't terrible because Alex is so blond. But there are three wiry hairs growing out of his chin that would support a full-size tire swing.

How would all this happen? Alex has survived without a girlfriend for seventeen years. Why is it so suddenly unbearable just because I'm in a relationship?

I came over with the intention of asking him to phone Kendra for me. But all of a sudden it doesn't seem like such a good idea.

That Monday, I get to school earlier than I've ever arrived there before. And at that, I have to hold myself back the last half hour. The librarian isn't in yet, but one of the custodians opens the media center for me. I boot up a computer and pass the time sifting through the latest offering of moronic ads on Meow Marketplace.

I'm placing this ringing endorsement on Madame Curie, a cat I found four years ago at Winn-Dixie. $300—PZ.

I try to look at it with Kendra's analytical eye. Yes, the price is ridiculous. Who has the gall to ask three hundred bucks for a stray he rescued from a supermarket? The key numbers are there:

$300 and four. There's the weird name. And ringing endorsement is a term that has come up before.

> **This is a double sale of two cats, first Material Girl, and second, Look Out Below. You've never seen such a pair of sharpshooters. $350—MK.**

How can a cat be a sharpshooter? Unless he can barf up a fur ball with deadly accuracy. Maybe it really is a coded message. But from who to who? And the biggest question of all: what is it doing on my Web site?

Normally, this would be enough to keep me tearing at my hair for the better part of a week. But this morning I've got one eye on my watch. Kendra's bus usually arrives at 8:05. I want to be the first thing she sees at school today so she knows that the reason I haven't called all weekend is not that I'm blowing her off.

I cover my face because I'm pretty sure my expression is one-hundred-percent goofy. After Friday, there can be no doubt in her mind that she's the A-1 priority in my life.

I position myself carefully so I'm right in front of her locker when she appears in the hall.

"Hey, you." I move to kiss her, but she sidesteps me, and I end up brushing my lips across her backpack.

"My cell phone died," I explain hastily. "I went by your house a few times, but I couldn't catch you outside."

She opens her locker and begins stowing books.

"I should have a new one tonight," I continue. "Tomorrow at the latest."

"Great," she says. It sounds like the wind off an iceberg.

I'm getting alarmed. "Kendra, what's with you? You know I always call when I can."

For the first time she looks at me. "Vince, it was fun. But I think we should stop seeing each other."

If she turned around and pushed a pie in my face, I couldn't be more amazed. "You're kidding, right?"

She shuts her locker. The metallic clunk reminds me of the slamming of a cell door in one of those prison documentaries. Harsh. Final.

I'm upset now. "It's the truth! You know why I have to use a bootleg phone."

She starts down the hall, then glares back at me. "This hurts twice as much as I thought it would! So just stop!"

"I can't show you the dead phone!" I plead. "I had to get rid of it!"

"Will you shut up about the cell phone?" she explodes. "It's not about the goddamn cell phone!"

I start to clue in. "It's about my father?"

"You lied to me!" she rages. "You said you had nothing to do with his business!"

"I don't!"

"I saw pictures!" she almost screams.

"That's impossible." I reach for her, but she bats my hand away.

"You're a loan shark," she accuses me.

"What?!"

"There's evidence! The FBI—my father—they've got pictures of you taking money from people! That sleazy guy from the parking lot, for one!"

When the pulse of horror has run its course through me, I'm left with a feeling that's sickeningly familiar. I had it when the cops locked me up for driving a birthday present I didn't know was stolen. And when I popped my trunk on Bryce Beach that night. It's the mixture of shock, queasiness, and understanding that comes with the realization that my last name has cost me something important. Again.

But this time the price is too high. "It's not what it looks like," I plead. "I'm *helping* those guys! They got in over their heads and came to me to put in a word with my father! But then I got sucked in too. . . ."

Even as I'm talking, part of me is listening through Kendra's ears. The fact is, I don't even believe myself, and I know I'm telling the truth. But my story sounds like a bad lie, and I'm tripping over my own facts as my mind struggles to recount the tale while at the same time processing some pretty big new information. The FBI has pictures of me. The FBI thinks I'm a gangster.

Kendra's crying now, and we're attracting a pretty big crowd in the preclass rush. A school the size of Jefferson is always good for a couple of breakups a week. But I never thought Kendra and I would be center stage.

"Shut up! Shut up!"

And I do, because at this point, I don't know what I'm saying anyway.

"Just—stay away from me!" she sobs, and runs off.

I'm almost crying myself. I *am* crying inside, but for some reason it just doesn't break the surface, as if Luca men are born with defective tear ducts.

It hurts so much, as if the weight of all the good times we've had together has just landed on top of me. I don't even consider going to first period. I head out to the parking lot and sit in my car, stunned and bitter. I curse Dad and Tommy and Ray and the uncles and their crews and all the connected guys who work for them. I double curse Jimmy and Ed for being so weak and stupid and drawing me into their mess. I curse the FBI for suspecting an innocent kid while ax murderers run free.

And that's when it hits me. The only question I haven't asked myself yet is the most important one: how did Agent Bite-Me find out about Kendra and me?

[SIXTEEN]

"**V**INCE, THE GUY'S AN **FBI** AGENT," Alex tells me. "We have to concede that he's got the skills to at least figure out who his own daughter's boyfriend is."

It's after school and we're in my Mazda, Alex at the wheel. I'm too distraught to drive. I've got the passenger seat in full recline, so I'm flat on my back, staring up at the sky through my leaky sunroof. The clouds are dark and lowering, just like my mood. A K-Bytes cassette plays on the tape deck, and every note from that throaty voice is like a piece of shrapnel in my abdomen.

Just the thought of no more Kendra has put a spring in Alex's step, and I hate him for it.

"You've got to be philosophical about this. With a girl like Kendra, you never should have had a chance to begin with, considering who your dad is. Face it, any action you get off an FBI agent's daughter is pure gravy, so you're way ahead of the game."

"You're enjoying this."

He's offended that I would even think such a thing. "When you bleed, I bleed," he insists. "It's my love life too, remember? You think I'm not feeling the pain?"

I *know* he's not feeling the pain.

"You'll never have a friend as supportive as me," he goes on. "As of today, I'm imposing sanctions on Kendra out of solidarity with you. She and I are finished as friends. She is a great singer, though," he adds, as my ex belts out "My Heart Will Go On" over the Mazda's tinny speakers.

"Yeah, I remember what a big fan you are," I snap. "Especially when you overdubbed her tape with 'Sounds of Bodily Functions.' That was a nice tribute."

Suddenly, there's a popping sound, and the song changes in mid-word. Now she's crooning "Yesterday."

I smile in spite of myself. When Kendra has something she wants to record, she'll pick up the nearest tape, jam it in the deck, and start singing. All the K-Bytes cassettes are like that, songs taped over songs, in the middle of songs, songs interrupted, and songs resuming partway through. Most people would take the time to put in a new tape, or at least forward to a blank part. But when Kendra wants to sing, it has to be now. For a girl who's normally logical to the nth degree, it's an attractive impulsiveness. At least it was in the good old days, before 8:06 this morning.

There's another clunk, and now she's halfway through "Hit the Road, Jack."

Alex brays a laugh. "Yeah, that's funny."

"You're supposed to be bleeding," I mumble.

Finally, we pull up in front of Alex's house. I get out and come around to the driver's seat.

Alex enfolds me in a bear hug. "We'll get through this, Vince."

"Let go of me before I kill you."

But when he scrambles inside, I realize that even Alex's company is better than being alone right now.

I start the car, but make no move to put it in gear. Going home isn't a good idea. I couldn't deal with Luca headquarters, with seeing Dad and Tommy.

But to be honest with myself, it wasn't even Dad and Tommy who sunk me this time. Kendra already knew about the family business. No, I did it to myself by getting involved in the seedy lives of Jimmy Rat and Ed Mishkin. I broke my own rule, and it cost me.

Savagely, I hit the eject button on the tape deck. K-Bytes pops out and lands at my feet. That cassette has something I could really use in my life: a rewind/erase function.

I replay it in my mind a hundred times: Jimmy Rat approaching me in the school parking lot, and me telling him to shove it.

But even knowing what I know, how could I have turned my back on Jimmy and Ed when they needed me? I wouldn't turn my back on them now if it wasn't for the fact that I have no choice. Thanks to Dad, those guys don't even dare talk to me long enough for me to warn them that the Platinum Coast is a sham.

After all my scrambling, my frantic phone calls, my trip to the city, those poor guys are in every bit as much trouble as they were before I started "helping" them. And I'm out six hundred dollars and one girlfriend for my troubles. Not to mention that the FBI is investigating me as a loan shark.

In the golden age of screwups, this will make the top-ten list. And the sad part is I'm sitting here like a spectator, watching it all unfold, and there's still nothing I can do about it.

Or is there? The idea hits me with such force that my whole body jumps, and I bang my knee against the steering wheel. It isn't even *my* idea, technically. It came from Jimmy and Ed. They wanted me to talk to Boaz and use my name to convince him that I speak for my dad. Well, I can't get through to Jimmy and Ed anymore, but there's nothing to stop me from going to see Boaz myself as a "representative" of Anthony Luca.

I love the plan so much so fast that it's almost scary. Is it the recklessness brought on by getting dumped, the way some guys drive too fast when their love lives go toiletsville? I really don't think so. Boaz may be a thug, but he'd have to be a suicidal thug to lay a hand on Anthony Luca's son. I'm like a walking insurance policy. I could go to the White House and give the president a wedgie, and when the Secret Service comes at me, I just flash my driver's license.

The only downside I can see is that Dad will hit the ceiling if he ever finds out. But frankly, that relationship is not a priority with me today. And anyway, Dad told me to stay away from Jimmy and Ed. He never said anything about Boaz.

If I can go head to head with Boaz and use my dad's name to get Jimmy and Ed their money back, then they can pay off their debts and start fresh. That could save those guys' fingers and bones and great-aunts, even their lives. I may be a washout as a boyfriend and a Web master. I may be under federal investigation for loan sharking. But surely there's no more worthwhile achievement than helping people in trouble.

I put the Mazda in drive and point it at the Southern State Parkway. Thunder rumbles. If it's supposed to be an omen, I ignore it.

I don't relish another hour-and-a-half creep into the city, so I flip from station to station, getting traffic reports. All anybody seems to care about on the radio is a line of violent thunderstorms that's heading our way. It seems somehow fitting that this weather apocalypse is unleashed on the very day that Kendra and I break up.

All the other drivers must be heeding the forecasters, because there's practically no one on the road. I make it through the Midtown Tunnel in forty minutes. By the time I hit Thirty-Ninth Street, it's so dark that I've got my lights on, and the wind is blowing newspapers and candy wrappers all over the place. I'm worried that the Platinum Coast might be closed up, with this big storm coming. But no, there's the pink neon, tasteful and urbane as ever.

I park (leave it to Jimmy and Ed to invest in a business on the only street in Manhattan where you can always find a spot) and head for the mirrored door.

Once inside, my eyes are instantly drawn to the stage, but there are no dancers. And anyway, the biggest guy in the world materializes in front of me within a second or two.

"Beat it, kid."

I give him what I hope is my father's stare. "I need to talk to Boaz."

The welcome wagon is unmoved. "When your zits clear up. Take a hike."

"The name's Vince Luca."

And the mountain is suddenly a molehill. "He's with Rafe over at the bar."

I take a couple of steps and freeze. Two men are perched on bar stools, deep in conversation. Boaz is a Middle Eastern–looking guy with curly hair and a dark tan. The reason why I know it's him is because I recognize Rafe. I know him as Rafael. Remember Johnny from my one and only football game? Well, Rafael is his dad. He also happens to be a member of Uncle Uncle's crew. And Uncle Uncle is under Uncle Carmine. And all of them are under Anthony Luca.

The kick in the pants sizzles all the way up my spine and rattles my pituitary. The Platinum Coast—the scam—it's a Luca operation!

I turn tail and run out of there before either man sees me. I feel dazed, as if I've taken a physical blow. I don't know what I expected, but it definitely wasn't this. I turn it over in my mind, but it always comes up the same way: Jimmy and Ed are falling behind in their debts to Anthony Luca because their money is being drained by a con game sponsored by Anthony Luca. Talk about a lose-lose situation!

I've had issues with my father's business before. I've seen him accused of a notorious homicide, for God's sake! But this has to take the prize. To steal someone's money, and then be coldhearted enough to send enforcers over to inflict vicious harm when he can't pay you, that's . . .

Tears are streaming down my cheeks. I couldn't cry over losing Kendra, but this has me blubbering like a baby. I guess it's just that I never saw my father as a bad person. Sure, I knew he was behind a lot of criminal activity, but I never thought he was intrinsically rotten. Until today.

I'm out of options. I've got to go home and face down my father over this. I don't know if it'll do any good, but my plan is to keep screaming until I get my point across. Luca communication skills.

But first I have to warn Jimmy and Ed not to hand over one more cent for the beautification and support of the Platinum Coast. That might be the hardest task of all, because both those guys have been threatened to stay away from me.

The rain starts on the way down to Java Grotto. This adds a ticking clock to my mission. If this storm is as big as the weathermen say, I've got to get my Mazda into some kind of shelter before Noah's flood comes through the cracks in my sunroof.

Bad luck: Ed isn't there. Even the bimbo hotline has been left unattended.

"Listen," I ask the girl behind the counter, "I need to find this club. Have you ever heard of a place called Return to Sender?"

She hasn't. I get blank stares from the customers too, until one guy waves me over to his corner table. Mohawk, pierced tongue, fish scales tattooed on his arms and neck. A real fashion statement. He gives me directions to Jimmy's club on

Norfolk Street, finishing with a single piece of advice: "Bring a bodyguard."

When I get there, I can see what he means. Return to Sender is a basement; *dungeon* might be a better word. The stairs that lead down into the bowels of New York City are littered with broken glass. The smell is a mixture of vomit and cigarettes. On the door is scratched something that, if anyone ever said it to you, you'd have to go into therapy for years. There are no windows, no signs; just a piece of paper covered in grubby Saran wrap nailed into the brick wall, reading WE CARD.

The rain picks up, puddling in the garbage at my feet. I can see flashes in the western sky, lightning over New Jersey.

I push open the heavy door and step inside. There are a few customers at the dingy tables—bikers, punks, and some of the stranger goblins from *The Lord of the Rings*.

Business is slow, and Jimmy Rat is sitting with one bare foot up on the bar, clipping his toenails into a cracked cup marked TIPS. When he sees me, he pitches a fit. "Jeez, Vince, get the hell out of here!"

"I need two minutes, Jimmy. That's all." But when I take a step toward him, he bolts. It's a funny hopping gait since he's only got one shoe on, and there's glass on the floor in here, too.

"Hear me out!" I cry.

He scrambles headlong into the bathroom. I try to follow, but he's holding the door against me.

"*One* minute!" I plead.

"You got something to say that's worth my life?" he snaps back. "'Cause that's what it's gonna cost!"

Suddenly, the door flies open, and I burst inside, just in time to see him disappear into a stall.

"Fine!" I exclaim. "We'll do it this way. You don't have to see me."

"I'm not listening!" he shouts, his hands covering his ears. Then, when I start talking, he sings "The Star-Spangled Banner" at the top of his lungs.

It's a Cirque du Soleil experience. I'm in the toilet of a club that's a toilet to begin with, so it's actually more like toilet squared. I'm yelling at a stall door that's singing the national anthem back at me while the storm of the century approaches from the west.

I climb up on the sink and stare down at this cowering singing idiot. He won't look at me, and he won't shut up, so I just say my piece at top volume right through the rocket's red glare.

"THE PLATINUM COAST IS NEVER GOING TO TURN A PROFIT BECAUSE IT'S NOT A REAL CLUB! THE WHOLE THING'S A CON, JIMMY! YOU AND ED HAVE TO STOP PAYING BOAZ! I DON'T KNOW IF I CAN STRAIGHTEN IT OUT WITH MY DAD, BUT I'LL TRY!"

"'O, say, does that star-spangled banner yet wave. . . .'"

Outside, a deafening crash of thunder. I can hear heavy rain pounding at the single window.

I'm screaming with frustration. "JUST NOD YOUR HEAD OR WAVE YOUR HAND IF YOU HEARD

WHAT I SAID! I'VE GOT TO GET HOME! THERE'S
A BIG THUNDERSTORM ON THE WAY!"

A sudden silence. Jimmy looks up at me. "With lightning?"

I have no patience left. "No, with ketchup! Of course with
lightning! It's a bad storm! The whole city's talking about
it! If you'd climb out of the sewer once in a while, you'd
know that!"

He looks up at me, his face intense with excitement.
"Gotcha, Vince! Thanks a million! I'll pass the word to Ed!"

I just naturally assume he means my business advice, and
not my weather report.

How the hell was I supposed to know?

By the time I get home, I might as well have been riding in a
convertible. I'm drenched, and there must be three inches of
water on the floor of my Mazda.

Mom sends Dad into the hurricane to move one of the
Mercedes out of our quadruple garage to make room for my
car. Two seconds on the driveway and he's every bit as wet as
I am.

Wet or dry, I'm revolted by the sight of my own
father. The word is out before I can bite my tongue:
"Bastard!"

He freezes, and we stand glaring at each other in the
downpour.

"Honest Abe Luca!" I growl in disgust. "What a crock!"

His response is measured. "As a parent, I never thought
I'd say this, but I sure hope you're drunk."

"You know who's ripping off Jimmy and Ed so they've

never got the money to pay you? You are!"

His eyes shoot sparks. "You've got some set of balls!"

"I saw it with my own eyes! One of the partners is Rafael! Uncle Uncle's Rafael! Which means some of that money trickles upstream to you!"

He's in a fury that the rain is doing nothing to cool. "Do you know how many guys I've got under me? Maybe you expect me to make notes every time somebody takes a whiz, but that's not how it works! These people have to make a living. And how they do it is their problem, not mine!"

I can get just as mad as he can. "Don't tell me you didn't sign off on this!"

"If it's Rafael and his guys, then Uncle signed off on it. Or maybe Carmine. You think they call the Pope every time there's algae growing in the holy water at St. Bart's?"

"Fine," I growl, flipping my wet hair out of my eyes. "You didn't know. But you know now. What are you going to do about it?"

A flash of lightning illuminates his face, and I can see what everybody else is so afraid of. Anthony Luca, mad, makes the storm of the century look like light rain.

"What I do or don't do is none of your business!" he roars. "Why should I have to take my cues from an overprivileged puke who looks down his nose at me and how I put bread on the table? Oh, Vince doesn't approve of The Life. Alert the media."

"I accept what you do," I throw back at him. "But what's happening to Jimmy and Ed—illegal isn't the half of it! You don't rob a guy and then break his legs because he's got no money. Surely there's some kind of honor code out there, even for people like you!"

He goes ballistic. "For someone who doesn't want any part of my business, your little nose is in pretty deep! I've got captains who put in less time than you!"

"I thought you wanted motivation," I say bitterly.

He seems genuinely anguished now. "What am I going to do with you, Vince? You're like crabgrass! Every time I turn around, you're in another part of the lawn!"

The next shot is mine, but I don't take it. All of a sudden, I'm completely spent, soaked to the skin and exhausted by a day that started in front of Kendra's locker, long, long ago, in a galaxy far, far away.

Twenty minutes later, we're both in dry clothes, and my mother is stuffing us full of lamb chops, warning, "A good dose of double pneumonia will put you totally out of commission." Agent Bite-Me, wherever he's listening from, will never guess that Dad and I were just at each other's throats. He can't see that Mom has placed us at opposite ends of the table, and is patrolling the demilitarized zone with a meat fork.

It's only now, when I can't say it because the walls have ears—that I realize what I should have told Dad out there. That this isn't same fight, new day. This is different. A line has been crossed, and I can never look at my father in quite the same way again.

[SEVENTEEN]

I'M AT SCHOOL BRIGHT AND EARLY AGAIN the next day, waiting on the doorstep for a custodian to let me in.

It's the same guy from yesterday. "Don't you got no home?" he quips.

Not much of a joke, but it's eerily close to the truth. I have a home, but there's a cold war going on there. I don't relish the idea of hanging around so Dad and I can glare at each other.

When Alex arrives an hour later, he finds me perched on a chair, putting up a large homemade poster. I jump down so he can read the message:

VOTE VINCE & KENDRA
FOR A ROYAL HOMECOMING

He's confused. "I don't get it."

"I don't, either," I sigh. "But she's the only thing in my life that makes any sense right now. I've got to get her back."

Alex makes a face, but it isn't his usual toxic look of distaste for all things Kendra-esque. There's something else in the mix. Maybe a little guilt?

"Don't even start," I groan. "I know you don't like her."

"I like her—" he protests.

"Then you don't like me and her," I persist. "Listen, I understand. Really, I do. But I have to try this, get her attention, put myself close enough to her that one day, maybe, she'll realize I'm not my father." I shrug miserably. "I'm going to go make some posters."

Wordlessly, Alex opens his locker, which is right next to mine. There, under his backup gym sneakers, sits a stack of continuous form paper. I recognize it immediately. It's a whole pile of those computer-generated Vince and Kendra signs, the ones I spent half the semester ripping down!

I stare at my friend since elementary school. "That was *you?*"

A shamefaced shrug; a tiny nod.

"Why?" But I already know. He figured I'd blame the posters on Kendra, which I did. And any disharmony between Kendra and me is beautiful music to Alex.

"I'm toe-jam," he admits, his face flushed. "You think I like it that I can't feel good for my own best friend? But I'm dying here! I think about sex twenty-five hours a day, and I can't even get a lunch date. Okay, I joke about it, but when the laughing stops, it really hurts! Especially when Tony Soprano's son, who doesn't even care, is so irresistible that even the FBI's daughter can't keep her hands off him!"

I glare at him. "You didn't place an anonymous phone

call to Agent Bite-Me, did you? You know, to talk about the weather, and who his daughter's boyfriend happens to be?"

He's genuinely distressed. "God, Vince, never!"

The weird part is I instantly believe him. Alex is a termite, not a saboteur. He wouldn't dynamite my relationship; he'd just chew away at it, hoping that the whole thing would fall apart on its own.

"I'd punch you," I growl, "but I'd probably break my hand on that obelisk you call a nose."

He looks mournful. "I'm not saying what I did was right."

"Well, what *are* you saying?"

"I'm not saying anything!" he snaps. "Except that I'm sorry and life sucks."

"I found that out yesterday," I agree sourly.

"And, hey," he adds, "free posters."

I can't stay mad at him. I never could. We haul out the computer-generated signs. There are twenty-one of them.

"Enough to get us elected president and first lady."

"Are you kidding?" scoffs Alex. "You guys are going to come dead last."

"I'm counting on it," I tell him. "Anyway, there's only one voter I'm trying to reach."

There's no way Kendra can miss all those posters, but she's ignoring me just the same. I catch glimpses of her as the day goes on—in crowded hallways, across the cafeteria—but every time she sees me, she quickly looks away.

I don't push my luck by trying to talk to her. Time heals all wounds.

"Figure two thousand years, and all is forgotten," Alex offers by way of comfort.

"You're way too cheery for a guy with a dead Chia Pet," I say, glowering.

The big news that day happens in cyberspace. Sometime last night, in the middle of the thunderstorm, that giant among Web sites, ILuvMyCat, nudges CyberPharaoh out of first place to become the most hit project in New Media class. I get a round of applause when Alex and I enter the computer lab. Even Mr. Mullinicks gives me a congratulatory slap on the shoulder.

"There must have been a big toga party down at the cat pound," I mutter, booting up a machine.

Sure enough, my site now boasts over a thousand hits, and there are 276 ads on Meow Marketplace. If ILuvMyCat holds its lead, I'm going to get an automatic A++ in New Media. And the irony is that I understand what's happening here less than anything in my entire school career, except maybe *Beowulf.*

I check the postings that put me over the top. "Aw, come on!" I blurt out. "Who calls a cat Compassionate Conservative?"

Fiona speaks up. "Maybe he's named after the horse."

I'm instantly alert. "There's a horse named Compassionate Conservative?"

"It was on the news last night," she replies. "The poor thing broke its leg in the middle of a race, and they had to shoot it. It was really sad."

Could this cat really be named after a racehorse? I read the ad again:

Cat for sale: Compassionate Conservative. You'll have a sixth sense about this cat. A real winner at parties, toga included. $350—TC.

Right after class, I head for the library and grab a copy of the *New York Post*. I flip through the sports pages, and there it is—a small article next to the race results: "Tragedy struck in the home stretch of the sixth race at Saratoga yesterday."

I look up, frowning. I can't escape the feeling that I've read this before. But that's impossible. I haven't seen a newspaper today. And even if I had, I sure wouldn't have looked up the racing results—". . . the sixth race at Saratoga . . ."

You'll have a sixth sense about this cat. A real winner at parties, toga included . . .

An "oof!" escapes from me as if I've just landed hard. I get some strange looks, but I can't worry about that. I feel like the scientist who figured out the Rosetta stone and decoded hieroglyphics once and for all.

"Toga": Saratoga Raceway.

"Sixth sense": the sixth race.

This isn't an ad to sell a cat! This is a bet on a horse! It's $350 on Compassionate Conservative, running in the sixth at Saratoga, placed by someone named TC. *A real winner* must mean the bet is for the horse to win.

My mind runs through an inventory of those other messages. The words *win*, *place*, and *show* are everywhere. *This is a real show-cat*, or *place this cat at the top of your to-do list*, even *a cat I found at Winn-Dixie*. Then there's the daily double: *this is* a *double sale of two cats*. Or the exacta: *I'm selling exactly two of my cats*. And Kendra was dead right about the numbers being important. They give the amount of the bet and which race it's on.

The names! Compassionate Conservative, Cuppa Joe, Color Me Purple, Thank-You Mary, Lip Gloss: they are all there in the race listings.

I go over every inch of that racing page with a fine-tooth comb. I'm not that easily amazed. Once you've popped your trunk and found Jimmy Rat bleeding into a blanket, everything else counts as relatively predictable. But the harder I look, the more I realize there's a whole secret language in Meow Marketplace, one that you practically need the Enigma decoder to figure out.

By matching the horses in the paper against a printout of the Web site ads, I painstakingly begin to identify the racetracks. *Toga* means Saratoga; that's the easy one. A *movie star* refers to Hollywood Park. *Pure gold* is Golden Gate Racetrack; *a gem of cat* is Emerald Downs. And *ringing endorsement* seems to be Belmont Raceway, as in *ringing* and *bell*. It gets cute like that. All those "inky" cats turn out to be running at Penn National Racetrack. And get this: the cats that can "quack" are at Aqueduct—like Aqueduck. It might be a joke, but I have a sneaking suspicion that your average track rat doesn't know any better.

But I might be selling them short, because some of these code names are kind of clever. *Sharpshooter* denotes Remington Park. Arlington International Raceway explains all those cats that enjoy long walks through the "cemetery." And my personal favorite: Churchill Downs is responsible for all those feline "prime ministers." Thank God that's straightened out. Now I can die.

That FBI heredity turns out to be worth something after all. The ads are exactly what Kendra said they'd be: coded messages. She didn't know that the code was for betting on horses, but she had the rest of it right. Sharp as a tack, my Kendra. Too bad she isn't *my* Kendra anymore.

There's only one loose end: who is the recipient of these messages? Who's taking the action from all these cyberspace horseplayers? I know the answer before I finish asking myself the question.

Who developed a sudden interest in the Internet in general and ILuvMyCat in particular?

Tommy Luca.

Here I am, so happy that my brother has found a hobby, and he's using it to turn my New Media project into an Internet betting operation.

Same old story. The vending-machine business has once again taken over who I am and what I do. I'm a prisoner in my own life.

The kicker, the real frustrating part in all this, is that there's nothing I can do about it. Mr. Mullinicks would just tell me it's my problem. The principal would probably call the cops. That leaves Dad, and he's Tommy's boss. Some of the profits from the operation end up in his pocket. Sure, I could get on my computer and delete the site entirely. But then I'd flunk New Media and miss starting college next fall. I'm trapped.

It occurs to me that my prospects for winning Kendra back are getting grimmer by the second. Remember, I'm not just a loan shark anymore. Now I'm a bookie.

I stand up to refold the *Post*. The front-page headline catches my eye: STORM WREAKS HAVOC ON AREA BUSINESSES.

I don't know what makes me read it. I had to bail out a Mazda Protege last night, so maybe I feel a brotherhood with other victims of the weather.

> Fires caused by lightning strikes destroyed three Manhattan businesses as a line of violent thunderstorms passed over the tristate area last night. Return to Sender on Norfolk Street, Java Grotto on West Broadway, and the Platinum Coast on West Thirty-Ninth Street were all gutted by flames. . . .

I come dangerously close to putting a secondhand burrito on the library carpet.

Jimmy's place! Ed's place! The Platinum Coast!

I feel like I'm reeling around the room, bouncing off the walls. I don't know what this is, but I know what it isn't: a coincidence! Lightning crackles over the city, and the only businesses that get hit are Jimmy's and Ed's? Impossible!

I run for the pay phone in the student common area. It

takes me a full minute to cram in forty-five cents, the cost of a call to New York. That's how badly my hands are shaking. The line rings and rings. Then it dawns on me: I only have their work numbers. If Return to Sender has been destroyed by fire, there's no phone left to answer.

In despair, I realize that I can't reach Jimmy or Ed. Going to the city won't help either. Their places of business are burned-out shells. Nobody's going to be there. And I don't know where else to look for them.

I rack my brain. Who would know how to reach Jimmy Rat? Certainly not the Avon Lady. Dad. Yeah, right. He's my favorite person, and I'm his. Uncle Shank—but he'll just tell Dad. Ray—that's the one.

I dial the Silver Slipper, and the bartender puts Ray on the line.

"I need a favor. Have you got Jimmy Rat's cell phone number?"

"Vince, are you nuts?" he exclaims. "There isn't a bagman in Hoboken who doesn't know that guy is off-limits to you!"

"Didn't you hear what happened?" I plead.

"I heard you and your old man had a real knock-down drag-out in a monsoon," he replies. "That's enough for me."

"Jimmy's club burned down," I go on. "Ed Mishkin's coffee bar, too. Along with some strip joint they both had money in."

"What's that to you?" Ray demands.

"I don't know! But it's something! I've got to get to the bottom of it!"

I hear him sigh. "Why do you think your father cut you off from Jimmy and Ed? He doesn't want you involved."

"I am involved!" I insist. "I couldn't be more involved! The FBI has pictures of me with those two guys! They think I'm a loan shark! I need that number!"

There's a long silence on the end. Then, "If this comes back to me, I'm going to deny it."

"I won't tell," I promise. "You won't regret this, Ray. You're the greatest."

He gives me the number.

It's normally so hard to get in touch with Jimmy that I'm caught off guard when he answers on the first ring.

"Don't hang up!" I blurt.

"Vince? Hang on a sec—I'll go someplace private." I hear voices and footsteps, and then it gets quiet. "I'm in the can at the Plaza. Me and Ed are treating ourselves to a big lunch to celebrate."

"Celebrate? Your bar got struck by lightning!"

"Yeah, Vince. I'm glad you called. Your advice worked out perfect."

"Advice?" I croak. "What advice?"

He laughs. "'There's a thunderstorm coming.' Gotcha, Vince. We talk about the weather all the time. You should see the circus geek they sent from the insurance company. He'd believe me if I told him I had the *Mona Lisa* hanging next to the dartboard."

Now that I've got the truth, I don't want it anymore. "You torched your bar for the insurance money?"

"Jeez, Vince. Is that any way to talk about an act of God?"

I'm hysterical. "You did! You did! And Ed too! And then you went up and finished off the Platinum Coast!"

"Funny thing about that," says Jimmy. "That must have been real lightning. We didn't want to be greedy. Just do our own places, pay off the sharks, and start fresh, like you said."

"Jimmy," I quaver, "when I said there's a storm coming, I meant, there's a storm coming! I have a leaky sunroof! I never told you to burn your club!"

"Yeah, whatever. But me and Ed love you, and we'll never forget what you did for us. You got the gift, kid, just like your old man."

I hang up on him. That last part hurts even more than the rest of it. To me there can be no greater insult than to be told I have a talent for my father's line of work. I make an innocent comment about the weather, and two grown men burn down their livelihoods!

I don't ever want to be good at this. You have to be a mobster first and a human being second. Look at how Dad defended Rafael and his scam even to me, his own son. And Tommy. What kind of brother would turn a high-school project into an illegal bookie operation? Only Ray is a real person. And even with him, I had to whine about the FBI snooping on me before he'd give me Jimmy's number against Dad's orders.

A funny feeling comes with that last thought, that there's something I should be noticing, but it's just outside my field of vision.

Maybe it's this: whenever someone mentions the FBI, my father, Tommy, the uncles, you can see the hair stand up on the back of their necks. But Ray didn't utter a peep when I told him the feds had pictures of me. I don't expect him to go berserk; Ray's no Tommy. But wouldn't he at least ask how I know a thing like that? I mean, I didn't tell Ray who Kendra's father is. He never even met her. He only saw her for a few seconds across a crowded restaurant that night at Topsiders. . . .

Right before Agent Bite-Me found out about Kendra and me . . .

What follows is a moment of terrible, yet perfect, clarity. I see my future, and I'm meddling in my father's business again. I have no choice. Because I know two things nobody else does:

1) The FBI really does have an inside man in the Luca organization, and
2) The inside man is Ray Francione.

[EIGHTEEN]

Ray Francione lives in a large two-bedroom apartment in a prewar building in Forest Hills, Queens. I've only been there once before, when Ray took me to the city and schmoozed me into a sold-out Limp Bizkit concert, front row seats, backstage passes.

That memory, as close to a warm fuzzy as you can get around the vending-machine business, sparks an odd mix of emotions. Betrayal, sure. For years, someone I considered my friend was living a lie. But there's a feeling of vindication too. How many times did I wonder how a great guy like Ray could be in The Life? Now I've got my answer. He never was.

I go early so I don't miss him, and he's still in his bathrobe when he answers the door.

"Vince, come on in. What, you fell out of bed this morning? Or are you still up from last night?"

"I'm taking a mental-health day off from school."

He says, "I'm keeping my eye out for a new cell phone for you, but there's not much around. Supply and demand."

"I don't need it anymore," I tell him. "Kendra and I broke up. But I guess you know that already."

He blinks. "That's too bad, kid. I had no idea."

I just keep talking. "You know because her father is your boss. And when you saw her at Topsiders, you had to give him a heads-up on who his daughter's boyfriend is."

I've got to hand it to him. He stays cool, the way an undercover agent should. Only his eyes give him away. They're alert, following my every move and gesture, very different from the "Who cares?" affect of most wiseguys, that veil of lethargy over repressed violence.

"That's crazy, Vince. I'm under your old man."

"Please—*don't*," I tell him. "I know what I know."

He glances at the door as if waiting for Tommy or one of the uncles to burst in, shooting.

"Nobody's with me," I say. "Nobody knows."

"This has to stay between you and me," he confides, "but your father's got me working with him special, smoking out this rat, and we're pretty sure it's Two-Ton Mike Falusi from your Uncle Carmine's crew. Now, I know what you're thinking. Mike's nobody. But you know how Carmine loves to talk—"

"No."

"Gotta be Mike." He's losing some of his coolness now. "Remember he got pinched smuggling smokes up from Virginia? He was with the feds for two days. That's when they must have turned him."

He sounds so reasonable that I actually find myself looking for ways to believe him. What am I, stupid? The evidence is right in front of my nose!

"I know it's you."

And then I see the pistol in his hand, pointed at my chest. I'm not sure how it got there except that it must have been a lightning move, because a second ago it was nowhere to be seen.

I guess part of me always knew this was possible. If I messed with my father's business long enough, sooner or later I'd end up staring at the business end of a gun. But after surviving the Jimmy Rats and the Boazes of this world, I never expected it to come from the one guy in all this who I thought was my friend.

The explosion of adrenaline exits via my extremities, leaving me with nothing but cold, clammy fear. My voice trembles along with the rest of me. "If you're telling the truth, you've got nothing to be afraid of."

"People in my business are very antsy about rats! I wouldn't be the first to get clipped just in case! Then, when I'm in the ground, they find out it's Mike after all, and, oops, too bad."

"You can't shoot me, Ray," I say slowly. "You're one of the good guys."

"You're meddling in matters that are none of your business!" he shouts. "And you're going to get yourself whacked!"

"Not by the FBI." Breathing a silent prayer, I take a cautious step forward.

His arm is rigid, but the gun is shaking in his hand. "I'll pull this trigger! I don't care who your old man is!"

The thought that a half-inch twitch of Ray's finger could end my life has completely shut down my brain. I don't know if I'm right anymore. I can't access any of the facts that led me to conclude that Ray's FBI. I'm flying blind, but I take another step, not out of courage, or instinct, or even stupidity. I'm propelled by a voice inside me, somewhere below gut level, that keeps repeating: *This is Ray. He won't hurt you.*

All at once, he lowers the pistol. "Three years," he says to no one in particular. "Three years I had in this operation. A year with Cosimo before that. And along comes a seventeen-year-old kid, and—" He makes a gesture with the gun that's so helpless, so harmless, that the weapon might as well be a peacock feather.

The sudden release of tension turns my bones to rubber, and I sit/collapse into a leather chair. I don't think football practice ever got my heart rate up this high. Ray's head is in his hands, and neither of us speaks for a long time.

Finally, I break the silence. "I used to look at you and think, Ray's in The Life, and he's a terrific person. Maybe they're not all bad. That's the most disillusioning part of this. Not that you're a fed, but that my poster boy for mobsters turns out to be a fraud, and that Dad and Tommy will never be like you."

"Your father's a remarkable man," Ray says sharply. "He brings a lot of integrity to a sick game. In a way, it's going to be a shame when he goes down, because, guaranteed, the next guy's going to be a whole lot worse."

"Dad's not going down, Ray," I say softly. "You are. You're not in any danger, but you're out of business as of now. I don't know what the FBI's going to do with you, but you don't work for the Lucas anymore."

He shuffles uncomfortably. "You're not an idiot. You know what this means to your old man, to Tommy. To Pampers. Witness protection—it's good, but they can't put you in another galaxy."

"You don't have to worry," I assure him. "I can't explain why, but Dad's not going to look for you." To his questioning expression, I add, "I've found some leverage."

"You'll excuse me for not believing you," he mutters. "This is my *life* here."

"I understand. But I repeat: you'll be fine."

He regards me with a new respect. "You're all grown up, aren't you?"

I shake my head. "I'm out of my league, which isn't such a bad thing, come to think of it."

"What if I said we've got you, too?" he ventures. "Your cell phone was a Bureau phone, and every word you said is on tape. Do you really want to go to jail for your family's crimes?"

"No way," I reply. "If Agent Bite-Me had tapes, he'd have known about his daughter months ago because she'd be on them. Besides, you wouldn't do that to me. You know I'm clean."

"Did you ever consider a career with the Bureau?" he suggests. "A guy with your bloodline could wipe out organized crime in this city."

"And wipe out my family in the process."

"You know it's the right thing to do," he persists. "If you didn't, you'd have Tommy's job by now."

"I know it's right," I concede. "But I was born on the other side."

"That's a cop-out. You've got a duty as a citizen. As a human being—"

I interrupt him. "We made it this far in the conversation. Let's not go backward. Especially not to the part with the gun. Once is my limit for wetting my pants on any given day."

He nods unhappily, scanning his surroundings. "I sure hate to leave this place. Rent control. Want the lease?"

"Are you kidding?" I retort. "I'm picking a college as far from my family as you can get without falling off the edge of the earth."

He laughs mirthlessly. "In that case, I'll probably see you there."

This hypothetical reunion, which both of us know will never happen, drives home the reality that this is good-bye.

"Before you go," I manage, grasping for the right words, "how bad is it? Dad's business, I mean."

He looks grave. "What, you want me to tell you they're lovable scoundrels? You know better than that. It's all-the-way bad."

"Murder?"

"Sometimes. Not as much as in the movies."

"What about the Calabrese hit? It was Dad, right? Just like everybody says."

"No," he replies. "Not Calabrese."

I'm surprised. "How can you be so sure?"

"Because we know who did it, and it wasn't him."

I'm astonished. "So why don't you arrest the guy?"

He's tight-lipped. "You wouldn't want that."

"Of course I want that!" I explode. "Murder is illegal for

everybody, not just the Lucas! Do you have any idea how much heat we've taken because of this thing? I can't clip my nose hairs without a team of agents listening in on the *snip-snip*! And all this time you know about the real killer and you're letting him go free?"

In answer, Ray gets up and rummages around a closet, producing an audiocassette marked 11/19/93 in Magic Marker. He pops it in the tape deck of his stereo and hits play.

The smooth, creepy voice I hear first belongs to Uncle Pampers, weekend yodeler and button man. He's talking about someone named Cel, and how, with him gone, Dad isn't safe from Calabrese and his crew.

"Cel is Celestino Puzzi," Ray explains. "Real old-school Mafia. To the day he died, he never drove a car; never had a phone. We couldn't touch him. Your dad and Calabrese worked for him."

I nod slowly, taking in every word. I realize that I'm hearing the true inner-circle machinations of my father's business, stuff even Tommy doesn't know about. This is the ultimate decision: who lives and who dies. I'm repulsed, but fascinated too, compelled to listen the way you can't look away from a car accident. I try to imagine nine-year-old Vince and Alex, still thinking girls are gross and Michael Jordan is God, shooting baskets in the driveway while this fateful meeting takes place.

According to Uncle Pampers, there will never be peace as long as Calabrese is "taking up space." Uncle Big-Nose, who's been spying for Dad from Calabrese's crew, has confirmed that they're ready to move against my father. "It has to be now," Uncle Pampers finishes, "Say the word, and this problem goes away."

I was right. It *was* Uncle Pampers. But I get no satisfaction from this realization as I hold my breath through a pregnant pause on the tape, waiting for Anthony Luca to give the order.

And it comes. But it isn't Dad who green-lights the most notorious mob execution of the last decade, although I recognize the voice immediately.

It's my mother!

"He won't touch this family!" she exclaims vehemently. "Pampers, I want that son of a bitch totally out of—"

There's a loud pop, followed by acoustic guitar, and someone sings:

> *"If I had a hammer,*
> *I'd hammer in the morning,*
> *I'd hammer in the evening,*
> *All over this land . . ."*

I freeze. The voice is a little higher, a little younger, but that's Kendra!

Eight years ago, Agent Bite-Me left this cassette on a countertop or a coffee table, and his daughter recorded karaoke over it! I have an instant replay of Kendra telling me about her father's Never-Bring-Work-Home policy, which started when some evidence was destroyed once. *Some evidence.* Yeah, tell me about it!

"You're probably mad at Kendra for dumping you," Ray

says gently, "but you owe her more than you'll ever know. If that song had broken in ten seconds later in the conversation, you'd be visiting your old lady in Leavenworth."

"Mom," I barely whisper. The order to take out Mario Calabrese came from June Cleaver! "If there's one person I was positive had nothing to do with all this—"

"She protected her family," Ray reasons. "The other choice was widowhood and fatherless kids. Calabrese had already given the contract to one of his people."

"Does Dad know?"

He shakes his head. "About Pampers, yes, but not your mom. And he knows he'd be dead if it hadn't happened. He hasn't been indecisive since. That's why, when he banned you from Jimmy and Ed, he came down hard. And everybody listened." He laughs mirthlessly. "Everybody except you, that is." He ejects the tape and tosses it to me. "Keep it. I hear you're a karaoke fan."

I stand. "I know it doesn't mean much under the circumstances," I say, "but I'm glad you turned out to be legit."

"It means enough." He reaches out and ruffles my hair. "Take care of yourself, kid. I'll miss you."

[NINETEEN]

I GIVE RAY FORTY-EIGHT HOURS to get out of town. He's gone in half that. I call the next morning to make sure everything's okay, and his phone is already disconnected. I guess that's one thing the Bureau is good at: making people disappear.

Funny—I'm the one who forced him away, yet I'm really counting on hearing his voice, even if it's just to tell me he's done packing and his plane leaves at eight. He's been like a big brother to me these last few years, even more than Tommy. I toy with the idea of our paths crossing again, but deep down I know it's never going to happen. Not as long as he's in the witness protection program, and my name is Luca.

I hear a bang followed by muffled cursing. The basement. Seven o'clock in the morning, and Anthony Luca, woodworker extraordinaire, feels the need to express himself through his art. I contemplate doing the cowardly thing, making a break for school without talking to him. I sigh. No, the confrontation is inevitable; he's going to notice Ray's disappearance eventually. And anyway, he's in the right place for a conversation.

As I descend the stairs, I see the project of the minute. It's a bookcase, and to my surprise, it actually looks like a bookcase.

Dad barely glances up from yanking twisted nails out of the back panel with his claw hammer. "Vince," he acknowledges with a grunt. The Cold War is still going strong at our house.

"Morning, Dad."

I press my hand against the side of the case. It's a casual leaning gesture, but what I'm really trying to do is rock it against the cement floor. It's perfectly stable.

I can't explain it, but somehow the thought that my father finally made a decent piece of furniture gives me strength to stand up to him. Almost as if the idea that he's not a total loss as a carpenter proves that he's not incorrigible as a mobster.

The logic is ridiculous. Of course he's incorrigible. The whole business is incorrigible. It's just so much *easier* than living a legitimate life. The money is better, the hours are shorter, the cars are nicer, and the perks (my mind travels to Cece) are unbelievable. But once you let the corruption in, you're shutting the door on your old self.

How do you struggle with a tiny paycheck when you know that huge sums of money are out there, yours for the taking? How do you wait in line when you could be escorted past the slobs to the best seat in the house? Take it from a guy who traded in a Porsche for a Mazda with a leaky sunroof. It's tough. Once you've taken that first perk, spent that first wad of fast cash, you're lost.

And that's not just for you; it's for everyone around you. My father is one of the top bosses in New York, and he couldn't keep his business off my back. The thought that my mother, the most straitlaced person who ever lived, ordered the hit on Mario Calabrese . . .

Oh, I understand why she did it. If Ray's to be believed, I'm even glad she did it. But we're talking about June Cleaver here! It proves that The Life isn't something you can order a la carte. If you're in, you're in all the way.

I know that means I'm corrupt too, because every dime that's ever been spent on me has been dirty money. But I intend to take advantage of one last piece of corruption, the A++ that I don't deserve in New Media, and which I'm only getting because of Tommy's Internet bookie scheme. I'm going to use that grade to get myself accepted to college far away from here, maybe an international program. It's the only way I'll ever stay clear of the vending-machine business.

"Got a minute, Dad?" I ask.

He flashes me a warning look. "This better not have anything to do with Jimmy Rat and Ed Mishkin."

"Cross my heart," I promise, knowing he's going to like this new subject even less.

He takes a seat in a wobbly chair and motions for me to do the same. "You know I'd never even heard of Ed Mishkin before all this? Now his name echoes in my head when I sleep."

The way he sits down registers with me as something of a shock. He sort of eases himself tentatively, almost like an elderly person. I blink. Anthony Luca isn't as young as he used to be! I have a bizarre feeling of thankfulness that he's got Mom to look after him so well. Then I remember with a shiver the lengths Mom will go to look out for her family.

Should I tell Dad about that, about who ordered the Calabrese hit? What would he say? He's as cool as they come, but surely that would shock him. If we were the Sopranos, he'd just smile with pride and say, "And she can cook, too!" and it would be this great TV moment, ironic, funny, and terrible all at the same time. But even for a Mob boss, television isn't much like real life. It would be a hard pill for him to swallow. Ever since I learned the truth, I can't shake a giddy vision of Mom in the kitchen throwing off her flowered apron just long enough to give Uncle Pampers the contract on Calabrese. Then back to the stove, where she whips up a delicious dinner.

No, this meeting has a purpose, and the only thing to do is get right to it.

"Dad, your inside man is Ray."

His head snaps to attention with a speed that would give a normal person whiplash. "What!" Then, a little less sure of himself, "How would *you* know?"

"For one thing, because he admitted it."

He stands, and there's no creakiness about him this time. "Do you have any idea what you're screwing with? If you're wrong—"

"I'm not."

"But if you are, it's something you can't take back! Don't you understand what has to happen now?" It's scary to see that much power caught off guard. "God—Ray! I never thought—there must be some way to know for sure."

"So you can kill him?"

"So I can do what has to be done to protect Brothers Vending Machines, which is none of your business!"

"You don't have to do anything," I assure him. "I've taken care of it."

He gawks at me, and I realize suddenly that, in this situation, *taken care of* has a very specific meaning.

"No!" I exclaim. "He left. He's in the witness protection program."

He's enraged. "You tipped him off?"

"I made a deal," I say. "He gets lost, and that's the end of it. You don't go looking for him."

"That's not your deal to make!" he storms. "And Ray knows it better than anybody!"

"It's a fair exchange," I insist. "You're free of a big threat, and he's off the hook."

"Who said life is fair? You know what life is? Cause and effect. You rat for the feds, you pay the price. Your deal doesn't change that. You want to make a deal with Ray that he'll jump off a bridge and fall up? Fine! But gravity won't honor your deal, and neither will I!"

"Well, you sort of have to," I tell him.

He gives me the Luca Stare with both barrels. "What happened? I died and left you in charge?"

If he doesn't turn off The Stare, I'm going to crumble, but I manage to say my piece anyway. "Tommy was using my Web site to run a bookie operation over the Internet. He could go to jail for that."

"You gave Ray evidence?"

I'm insulted. "Of course not. But if anything happens to Ray, that floppy disk is going to the FBI. And please don't ransack my room, or my locker at school. It isn't there."

The floodgates open, and the full force of his anger is unleashed. I can only hang on to my malformed chair as he hurls every curse in the book at me. In this white-hot fury, surely he's lost all trace of paternal feeling for me. At this moment, I'm any poor dumb slob who has crossed him, and my mother is the only thing standing between me and a landfill in Staten Island. It's possible that this very tirade has been, for some, the last thing they ever heard on earth.

Unbelievably, a calculating, almost Dadlike thought penetrates my misery as the onslaught continues to blast me: *This is the worst he can dish out.* And the corollary, surprising in its clarity: *This is the volley you have to return.*

So I say it as matter-of-factly as I can: "I've got the evidence, and you don't. Your words—'cause and effect': Ray's life—the disk."

I can feel the heat rising from his red face. "You'd turn in your own brother?"

That's a question I've prepared for. "Look at it this way, Dad. It's Tommy's book, but the Web site is in my name. So you won't just have one son in jail. You'll have two. But don't worry, I'm sure we'll be fine in there. After all, a guy like you doesn't have any enemies, right?"

He's speechless. I've never seen that before.

"Ray's like a brother to me, too," I add.

"He's rat scum!" he spits. "And you're an idiot! You never keep evidence around, even if you think you're the only person who's ever going to know about it! How would you like it if that disk fell into the wrong hands?"

"It won't," I promise, thinking of my secure hiding place. Last night when everyone else was asleep, I triple-laminated that disk in plastic and glued it down under the asphalt roofing tiles over our garage. The thing is, our house has a twenty-year roof, and it's eleven years old. So by the time the shingles are due to be replaced, the seven-year statute of limitations on Tommy's crime will be long expired. If our roof comes down and Agent Bite-Me himself finds the disk in the rubble, it will be useless to him. I say, "I've worked it out so it's good for everyone, and nobody gets hurt."

He snorts. "Listen to King Solomon here, fixer of all problems, dispenser of justice. Who do you think you are?"

"Anybody who could do what you did to Jimmy and Ed has no right to lecture me about justice!"

He pounds his fist on the bookcase, which, miraculously, doesn't collapse. "Jimmy and Ed! My favorite subject! For your information, Your Majesty, Jimmy and Ed are off the hook, which is a good thing!"

"It's still not justice," I point out. "Rafael and that guy Boaz robbed them blind, and a lot of other people too. But they get their insurance money, same as Jimmy and Ed."

My father casts me a superior smile. "You think so, huh? Well, it just so happens that they sold seven hundred percent of that place, and they're only getting insurance for one club. They've already come to me to borrow the money to pay off a lot of really angry people."

I'm confused. "Then why did they burn the place down?"

"Maybe someone else did it," he suggests dryly. When I don't clue in, he adds, "Maybe there's more than one King Solomon in this family."

Light dawns on me. That's what happened to the Platinum Coast! Jimmy and Ed took care of their own businesses, and the Platinum Coast fire was the fine hand of Anthony Luca. Because of that, the investors break even, and Rafael and Boaz get burned by their own scheme. It's the perfect solution; the only solution. And Dad found it, the way he always does.

He gives me an appraising look, and a small smile displaces some of that anger. "I don't know whether to kick you out of the house or hire you. I always thought the advantages you had made you a flake-in-training—no drive, no motivation, just take, take, take. I was wrong about you, Vince. I don't like what you did, but I've got to hand it to you, you're motivated."

"I can't work for you. You know that."

"Too bad," he says. "Look at what you've accomplished these last couple of months. You smoked out Tommy's book on your computer, you got Jimmy and Ed square, you blew the doors off the Platinum Coast, and you found an undercover agent right under my nose. There are a million guys who want to be in The Life. But real brains, that's something different."

"Most of it was luck," I shrug, embarrassed. "Bad luck. I definitely didn't tell Jimmy and Ed to burn down their places."

"Doesn't matter." He walks over to the desk and pulls out a fat envelope. "Your points, in advance."

"My points?"

"Insurance pays Jimmy and Ed, Jimmy and Ed pay me. Since you took care of those guys, you get a cut. I usually wait till I've got the cash in hand, but I figured, hey, I know where you live."

"I can't accept that!"

He rolls his eyes. "Fine. It goes in your college fund." At my surprised look he snaps, "Yeah, you've got a college fund, smartass, just like normal people! We're not going to pull up in front of Harvard with a suitcase full of Krugerrands."

"I'm amazed you didn't call it a *university* fund."

He waves the money in my face. "You sure you haven't got a use for some of this before I make the deposit?"

"I won't touch it."

"You've touched it already!" he shouts, rummaging through the drawer, and slapping a piece of paper down on the blotter.

I stare. It's a credit card bill, for my emergency card, the one from Banco Commerciale de Tijuana. There it is, my six-hundred-dollar cash advance—5,400 pesos—circled in angry red.

I'm caught off guard. In all the time I've been holding that card, never once did it occur to me that it was legitimate. I always assumed it was like the Porsche. Call me crazy, but I actually get a warm feeling that Dad's concerned enough about me to make sure my emergency credit card isn't hot. In my family, swag is so common that when something is bought and paid for the old-fashioned way, it's almost a Hallmark moment. It shows you really care.

"Sorry, Dad. I really was going to pay it back. I just got—sidetracked."

"Yeah," he finishes. "Making my life a living hell."

"Take it out of my—uh—cut." I frown. "There's only one thing I don't understand. Why Tijuana?"

"I own a piece of the bank," he replies.

I'm goggle-eyed. "Really?"

"I may not wear fancy suits, but I'm every bit as much of a businessman as those clones on Wall Street. A deal fell through, and this guy was left holding the bag. He didn't have the cash, so I took his shares in the bank. Happens all the time." He smirks at me. "Tell Jimmy and Ed they get a pass for the six hundred."

I guess my jaw drops, because he continues, "Think, Vince. Why else would you need it? You're a sharp kid who's getting sharper every day. But I want you to admit that you're not smarter than me just yet."

Suddenly, I know exactly how Barry Bonds must feel when someone pitches him a slow, straight fastball. "Right, Dad," I agree readily. "I'd better get over to school now. I've got to find Agent Bite-Me's daughter and try to get her to take me back. We've been dating for the last two months—but a smart guy like you must know that already."

It's such a perfect exit line that I don't even stick around to enjoy the look on his face.

[TWENTY]

Tal Obodiac and Astrid Martin are elected Jefferson High School's 2002 Homecoming King and Queen. Both blond, blue-eyed. She's a cheerleader and he plays football. You could switch them with the king and queen from any other school and nobody would even notice.

Alex knows a guy on the committee, so he does a little behind-the-scenes scouting for me.

"Three votes," he reports.

I'm equal parts impressed and horrified. "That's all we lost by?"

"That's all you got. Three votes."

"Oh, uh—great," I manage.

"That weird kid who ran with his cocker spaniel got forty."

I glare at him. "And I'll bet you were one of them."

He takes it personally. "I'm a worm, Vince, not a traitor. Besides, do the math. Three votes. You, me, and—"

I shake my head. "No way. Not Kendra. She wouldn't put

an X beside my name unless it was to send me to the electric chair."

"Hey," he says sternly. "You think it's easy for me to root for you guys? The least you can do is get back together."

"Because it's your love life too," I finish.

"No," he says seriously. "But look at it this way. If you of all people can b.s. an FBI agent's daughter into disbelieving her own father's photographic evidence, it has to bode well for the b.s. master who taught you everything you know."

Apparently, Galileo was wrong. Everything orbits Alex Tarkanian.

I can't find Kendra anywhere, and she isn't in the cafeteria at lunch. I'm starting to suspect that she heard about our last-place finish in the homecoming balloting and bolted. I mean, neither of us expected to win—and in view of our breakup, the last thing she'd want is to be my "royal consort." But to have your nobody-hood confirmed by school-wide vote in a very public forum—that has to hurt. I know I felt it.

I may be a dweeb in the eyes of the school, but in New Media at least, I get respect as the architect of the supreme site. I spend the class crafting a special message that will appear on ILuvMyCat whenever somebody tries to enter Meow Marketplace:

> **Due to overwhelming response, Meow Marketplace is no longer accepting new ads. Enter your five-digit ZIP code and click on the link below to visit the site of the Humane Society branch nearest your home.**

Let's see what Tommy has to say to that.

Mr. Mullinicks doesn't approve. "Not a smart idea, Vince. Meow Marketplace is the most successful feature of any site in the class. Without it, you've got practically nothing."

"That's the whole point," I say. "Maybe I can divert some business over to Feline Friends Network."

"It'll drastically reduce your traffic," he warns. "How can I determine your grade based on how many hits you *might* have gotten if you hadn't made this unwise move?"

I've been waiting an entire semester for that question. "With all due respect, Mr. Mullinicks," I tell him, "that's your problem."

I start toying with the idea of calling Kendra when I get home. Her dad will tape the call, but at this point, what harm can it do? That's the one advantage of hitting rock bottom: the situation couldn't possibly get any worse.

So I'm surprised to come around a corner and find her standing right in front of my locker, waiting for me, beautiful and terrifying and no longer mine.

She doesn't say anything, so I fire a cautious salvo. "We didn't win."

"I heard. Was it close?"

I shake my head. "We got three votes."

She absorbs the blow. It doesn't seem to bother her.

"I voted for us," I continue, "and I think Alex did, out of pity. I don't know who was number three."

"Me."

I just stare.

"Ray came by before he—left. He told me how you were

only trying to help those guys. How you protected him. I'm so sorry for not believing you."

My heart soars. I've been wrong about a lot of things these last couple of months. But I was bang-on about Ray Francione. I ruined a four-year undercover operation and got him banished to God-knows-where in the witness protection program, and he still took the time to visit my girlfriend and straighten everything out before he had to disappear, thanks to me. If that's a rat, I'm moving to the sewer.

"I want you back," is all I can think of to say.

"Me, too," she replies in her husky singing voice, the voice that kept Mom in the kitchen and the Calabrese murder an unsolved crime. We're in each other's arms now, the last-place finishers in the homecoming vote, making a scene at dismissal, the most crowded time of the day. We're such an unlikely pair, Mob prince and FBI princess, but we must look like a cliche: the classic locker-front break up/make up. From the double doors at the end of the hall, I catch a glimpse of Alex, flashing me V for victory.

Kendra becomes aware of the scores of eyes on us, and tries to wriggle from my grasp.

I don't let go. "They didn't vote for us. Screw 'em," I whisper.

She laughs and melts back into me.

"How's your father taking this?" I ask.

"He hates it," she admits. "What about your family? Do they know yet?"

"I just spilled the beans to my dad, but I didn't stick

around for the postgame fireworks. It's not going to be easy, for either of us."

She looks into my eyes and sighs. "What did Romeo and Juliet do?"

"They died," I remind her gently. "Some mix-up with the poison—"

She cuts me off. "But what if they'd lived?"

I think it over. "Same as us, I guess. Stay cool, and never bring the folks together for a meet-and-greet."

FIND OUT WHAT HAPPENS NEXT!

Now available wherever ebooks are sold.

LOOKING FOR MORE FROM GORDON KORMAN?

Turn the page to start reading!

[ONE]

On a scale of one to ten, this party was at least an eight. It was in full swing by the time we crashed it. Not that you can ever crash when you're with Todd Buckley. Todd's invited everywhere, and he brings who he pleases. Quarterback's privilege.

The carpet smelled like beer already, so I knew the festivities had been going on for a while. The stereo must have set somebody back a few bucks, because when the bass was cranked, you could feel the air move. The floor was moving too, under the stomping feet of a mob of dancers. Arms and legs jostled the shiny keg, which sat in a little kid's inflatable wading pool by the living room–dining room.

As we watched, Nelson Jaworski staggered in from the hall and hit the wading pool face-first in a tidal wave of ice and slush. There was a roar of laughter until the big lineman sprang back to his feet, snatched up the keg like it weighed nothing, and reared back to heave it through the picture window.

Todd and I joined the stampede to stop him.

"Take it easy, buddy," Todd soothed. "If you trash the keg, it means we're out of beer."

The logic was fairly straightforward, but what got through to Nelson was the fact that it was coming from Todd. "Yeah, yeah, I'm cool, I'm cool."

By that time, somebody had the brains to wave a full cup under his nose. He surrendered the keg into the arms of the three guys it took to set it back in the pool.

Todd was laughing as we pushed through the crowd. "What do you think, Rick? This is what you've been missing."

I worked as a camp counselor in the summer, so I skipped the first two weeks of football practice that our team always had before the start of school. I was a little out of the loop. "This guy Jake—he moved here while I was away?"

Todd smirked. "Coach thinks he dropped straight from heaven. He's a long-snapper. That's all he does."

"No way!" Coach Hammer didn't let anyone get away with doing only one job. Even Todd, his precious superstar, played nickel back and anchored the onside kick coverage team.

"No bull," Todd assured me. "Coach got sick of watching Nelson heave the ball twenty feet over your head, and now he's got a guy who does nothing but snap long. I'll introduce you."

I was the kicker and backup QB. Second fiddle to Todd. Story of my life.

Since I was with him, I was in on the endless procession of

high fives and backslaps that our quarterback seemed to draw like a magnet as we toured the party.

Everybody was there—most of the football team, their girlfriends, the cheerleaders and a bunch of their boyfriends and friends, the cooler people from student council, and a collection of athletes from basketball and track. I noticed some sophomore girls whose names I didn't know—they'd really filled out over the summer—and a few guys who played in their own rock band. It was the guest list that really made this bash what it was. If I could put together the party of my dreams—not that my parents ever left me alone in the house for more than five minutes—this was exactly the kind of crowd I'd want. I marveled at how a newcomer like Jake Garrett could waltz into town and instantly know all the right people to invite.

I turned to Todd. "Do you see him?"

Todd shook his head. "Must be upstairs."

"Don't his parents notice that there are fifty kids going nuts in their house?" I asked.

"Jake's dad's out of town five days a week," Todd explained. "His mom lives in Texas somewhere." He picked up a slice of pizza from a table that was loaded with the stuff, folded it expertly, and took a bite. "Last week," he mumbled, "I dared Nelson to do ten beers and ten slices in ten minutes. Puked his guts out from Mr. Garrett's bedroom window. Killed a rosebush."

I had to laugh. As quarterback and kicker, Todd and I entrusted our lives to Nelson on the football field. And he delivered. But off the field, it would take two of that guy to make a half-wit. Right now we could see him totally passed out on the living room couch. Someone had stuck a plastic daffodil up his nose. They never would have tried it if he had been awake.

I nudged Todd, but his attention was definitely elsewhere. He was having a little nonverbal communication with one of the sophomore girls. This was the real reason Todd loved these parties. It had nothing to do with who barf-bombed a rosebush. The ladies loved Todd, but not half as much as he loved them. Never mind that Todd had been going out with Didi Ray for over a year now. On a scale of one to ten, Didi was a twelve on a bad day. This sophomore was in the low sevens, tops. But the sophomore was here, and Didi was not. And mostly, Todd was Todd.

They began to close the distance between them, moving in that trancelike state that is so dramatic and all phony. It would have been a really romantic moment except for the three guys standing on their heads against the wall trying to chug upside down while a cheering section bellowed encouragement. I think they were betting on the outcome. My money was on more dead rosebushes.

Just when Todd was a few feet away from his quarry, a hand with painted red fingernails grabbed him by the collar and yanked him to one side. It was cheerleader Melissa Fantino, who was no more than a six. But certain parts of her were pretty much off the scale. She dragged Todd into the bathroom, then slammed and locked the door behind them.

I was amazed. Melissa was Nelson's girlfriend. Messing with her was like gargling nitro.

I waited for the bathroom door to open. This was a joke, right? Those two would come giggling out, busting my chops for being so gullible as to believe that something was really happening in there.

The door stayed shut. I sure hoped Todd knew what he was doing.

With the only main-floor bathroom out of service indefinitely, I headed upstairs in search of facilities. On the way, I passed two sleepers—one on the landing, and one draped across the top step. The second guy had a couple of friends with him, if you could call them that. They were laughing like maniacs while emptying a squeeze bottle of contact-lens solution into the poor kid's open mouth.

When I finally climbed over that obstacle, I had to revise my estimate of the attendance at this party. There were about twenty people packed into the hall alone. But while downstairs was wild and crazy, the second floor seemed to be the designated chill-out area. The range of conversations was amazing—everything from baseball to the meaning of life. A bunch of guys from the JV football team were reciting the first Austin Powers movie line by line. I can't imagine how the subject came up, but there was a group debating the merits of Canadian bacon versus regular ham for breakfast. The Canadian-bacon advocate was so impassioned that he looked like he was ready to start throwing punches if the argument didn't go his way.

I found what I thought was a bathroom door and threw it open. There was a high-pitched female scream, followed by an angry male voice: "Get out of here, man!"

Quickly, I retreated. I didn't know who the girl was, but the voice belonged to our fullback—after Nelson, the toughest kid on the team.

"Each year, the young salmon swim upstream, fighting the current, to spawn," came a deadpan voice behind me.

I wheeled. There, his face buried in an enormous bag of jalapeño-and-pineapple pretzels, sat Dipsy.

To this day I couldn't tell you his real name. We called him Dipsy—after the Teletubby, the green one with the phallic symbol growing out of his head—because he had a cowlick that stood straight up at attention. He said stuff like that all the time. You could never quite tell if he was serious, or if it came from whatever he was smoking. Although, to be honest, I never saw Dipsy smoking anything. It was just the simplest explanation for his weird personality and his perpetual munchies.

"Where's the bathroom?"

"Occupied," came the reply from the pretzels. His languid gaze traveled down the hallway of closed doors. "Everything's occupied. Except—"

Without standing, turning, or missing a bite, he reached over his shoulder and tried the knob behind him. Locked. The brass was shiny and unscuffed—obviously new. And there was a keyhole—it was made for a front door, not a bedroom.

"Our host likes his privacy," I commented.

"The great white shark is a solitary hunter, its isolation ensured by row upon row of razor-sharp teeth."

"You've got to get the cable company to take Animal

Planet off your TV," I advised, adding, "Is Jake a friend of yours?"

He shrugged. "Are you a friend of mine?"

In fact, the bizarre remark almost made sense. In a way, Dipsy was everybody's friend and nobody's at the same time. He was kind of the misfit on the guest list since he wasn't really popular, or on any team or club or anything like that. Yet he was always there, shoulder to shoulder with the jocks and cheerleaders, with his ripped-up jean jacket and his inventory of junk food. He never seemed to mind the players cracking on him, which they did mercilessly. One time at the mall, a whole bunch of them lifted up Dipsy's rusty Fiat and turned it sideways in its parking spot, locked in by two other cars. The poor guy had to wait three hours for the people on either side of him to leave. But he never complained, and he always came back. And nobody tried to keep him away, which was more than you could say for the way Todd and his crowd treated a lot of other kids.

"Of course I'm a friend of yours."

"Yeah?" He regarded me expectantly.

I guess I was supposed to present my resume to prove it. The truth was that, while I'd grown up with Dipsy, I didn't know him very well. Part of that was Dipsy's fault. He wasn't exactly Mr. Communication—except maybe to Jacques Cousteau.

I definitely wasn't his enemy. I didn't pick on him like the other Broncos. Once, back when we were sophomores, Dipsy really came through for me in a tough spot. Maybe I should have shown my gratitude a little more over the years. But

Dipsy didn't seem to care. He was always too busy talking about manta rays.

"You've got a million friends," I said finally. "We just can't find you hiding upstairs in a bag of pretzels."

He replied, "The remora bides its time on the coral reef, waiting for . . ."

I didn't stick around for the rest of it. Partly because I wasn't in the mood for *Waterworld*, but mostly because the bathroom opened up.

I had to run to beat out one of the *Austin Powers* cast. While I was washing up, there was an eruption of high-pitched screaming from the yard. I peered through the curtains. In the back, some football players had turned the hose on a couple of those sophomore girls.

I raced down the stairs and outside. I think kickers are natural team peacemakers, since coaches always send us in from the sidelines to intervene when the shoving starts. But when I got to the main floor, the two would-be firefighters—receivers on our team—had turned suddenly chivalrous. One was wrapping the waterlogged girls in throw blankets from the couch, while the other got them drinks. The keg was pretty low by this time, so while our tight end poured, this kid I didn't know pumped the handle on top to keep the beer coming.

I turned to the shivering girls. "You'll have to excuse my friends. They get a little carried away at parties."

I don't think they even noticed I was there. They were the center of attention, and they couldn't have been any happier about that. The kid at the keg poured himself a cup and then one for me too. "Here you go, baby."

I personally think beer tastes like sand, but I accepted the drink. The music was too loud to go into a long explanation, especially to a stranger. I checked out the newcomer. He looked like he'd just waltzed off the pages of the J. Crew catalog, or maybe Banana Republic. I mean, nothing he was wearing was all that special—just a plaid shirt, untucked, over a white tee and khakis. But everything went together perfectly, and hung on him with that rumpled casual effect that you can't get by being casual. This guy *worked* at it.

We were kind of the odd men out, since there was definitely a love connection in the works between the receivers and the soggy sophomores.

I guess he saw me eyeing my beer with distaste. "There's more to drink in the laundry room, baby," he told me. "Booze, wine, soda. The washing machine's packed with ice."

I was impressed. "This guy Jake throws quite a party."

At first he looked as if he didn't understand. Then he said, "I'm Jake."

"Oh, sorry!" Feeling stupid, I fumbled to shake his hand. "I'm Rick Paradis."

"Rick the kicker!" he exclaimed. "I'm your new long-snapper, baby. We're going to be working together on the Broncos!"

An arm appeared around each of our shoulders. "I see you guys are getting to know each other."

It was Todd, looking pretty disheveled after his interlude in the bathroom. Melissa, his partner in wrinkles and lipstick smears, was in the dining room with some other cheerleaders, sending burning glances in his direction.

"*A-choo!*" On the couch, Nelson sneezed the daffodil out of his nostril and shook himself awake.

In one quick motion, I tossed my drink in Todd's face and wiped the lipstick off his mouth with my hand. Nelson was pretty wrecked. But only one girl at this party was wearing lipstick the color of stale doggy-doo. He wouldn't have to be Einstein to put it all together.

"What are you, crazy, Rick?" Todd sputtered.

Nelson took one look at us and lapsed back into his coma.

I didn't know how much I could say in front of Jake, so I just muttered, "You've got to watch out for yourself, man."

Jake gave us a knowing smile, like this was some juicy conspiracy that only the three of us were in on. "The word is you've got the hottest girlfriend in town," he told Todd. "Rumor?"

"Didi's the real deal," I supplied.

"You should have brought her," Jake told Todd.

Our quarterback shrugged. "I can have Didi any time I want. Tonight's all about . . ." He let his eyes wander appreciatively around the room. "You sure give great parties, man!"

Jake turned to me. "How about you, baby? Got a girl-friend?"

I shook my head. "No."

"Because he's an idiot," Todd finished for me. "Didi's best friend, Jennifer—goes to school with Didi at St. Mary's—she loves this guy! Guess who wants to be just friends."

"Nothing wrong with that," put in Jake.

Todd rolled his eyes. "Listen, Didi and Jennifer are more than inseparable. They're like Siamese twins. Half the time, when I go out with Didi, I'm stuck with Jennifer too."

"So I have to date Jennifer to make you happy," I finished for him. "There's a great basis for a relationship."

"Basis, shmasis," Todd scoffed. "Jen's *hot*."

And she was. But not for me. Us being just friends—that was Jennifer's decision, not mine. Todd knew that better than anybody. He was the one who'd personally sealed the deal.

At that moment, a great laughing cheer went up in the house. I wheeled just in time to see Dipsy, in his underwear, running down the stairs in pursuit of three football players who had his pants. The crowd parted to make room for the thieves, who raised their catch over their heads like Olympic gold medalists running with the flag. Bellowing trumpet sounds, they tossed the Levi's up onto one of the blades of the living-room ceiling fan. Round and round went the jeans, legs dangling.

Dipsy made a couple of jumps at the fan, but Michael Jordan he wasn't. He disappeared into the kitchen and came back with a chair, all the while ignoring the dozens of people who were slapping and pinching his butt. When he finally got up there, someone cranked the fan to maximum speed. He made a couple of snatches, but his pants were whipping by so fast, he couldn't get the timing right. At last, he grabbed hold of a leg, overbalanced and fell into a pack of cheerleaders. Amazingly, they caught him—they practiced catching Melissa for their regular routine. But he was a lot heavier than she was, and the whole group keeled over under his weight. One girl conked her head on the edge of the pizza table, and her basketball boyfriend got mad and went after

Dipsy. The poor guy was hopping around, trying to get his jeans back on, while staying ahead of six-foot-three inches of outraged muscle. Plants got knocked over. Pizza slid off the table and onto the floor. Drinks were spilling left, right, and center as the pursuer and the pursued bumped and jostled everybody.

Todd slapped me on the back. "It's going to be a great senior year!"

Jake was watching the goings-on with unruffled calm. Like it didn't bother him in the slightest that his house was getting trashed. Very cool under fire, this new kid.

On a scale of one to ten, I bumped the party up to a nine.